JanIus Pawns Book I

D.L. Hannah

This work, including all names, characters, and incidents, are products of the author's imagination or are used fictitiously and are not to be construed as real. No identification with actual persons (living or deceased), places, buildings, and products is intended or should be inferred.

ISBN 9781965798164   2025

Contents

Isis, this is our third series. Three home runs in a row!

Chapter 1

"Sorry, Dr. Ascencio, we can't let you enter the building. Not without being scanned in."

Shifting his heavy leather backpack from one shoulder to the other, Justin sighed. "I have patients to see, Officer Sedgewick. We've been through this before. I'm not getting the chip."

Officer Sedgewick nodded. "I understand. But I have my orders not to allow anyone inside without it. The law must be followed."

Justin's lips thinned. "The law. Do you mean a bunch of silly executive orders that don't align with our constitution? You remember the constitution, right? Before a crazy president started ignoring it?"

Officer Sedgewick spread his feet apart and placed a hand on each side of his vest. An annoying gesture some cops did when they wanted to look important. It never failed to irritate Justin.

"Tell me, Officer Sedgewick, what's lawful about forcing people to get devices implanted under their skin just to work and eat? Five years ago, tourists enjoyed coming here. Even that's been blown to hell since the neo-Nazis took over. Now we're despised all over the globe."

The officer shifted nervously on his feet.

"I'm a brain surgeon. If I don't operate on patients, they'll die. How many more people have to die before we stand up and do something about this dictatorship? As of this morning, diseases we cured fifty years ago have killed over two hundred thirty thousand people. How can you stand there and be okay with this?"

Officer Sedgwick's face reddened. "Who says I am?"

He extended his arm, showing a long, slim scar traveling from his elbow to his wrist.

"I had to take the chip, Dr. Ascencio. If I didn't, guess what? My family doesn't eat. I've got two girls in school and one on the way. I'm not rich with a fancy education like you. You speak real nice, but thumbing my nose at President Musdin ain't an option!"

Justin sighed. "It would be very condescending if I said I understood, so I won't. You're right. I don't have to worry about money or a family to provide for. But it has to stop somewhere. Otherwise, there'll be nothing left for your children by the time they're our age."

Officer Sedgewick briefly hung his head, then looked up at him. "I'm sorry, Dr. Ascencio. I'm gonna have to take you in."

Justin knew what that meant. Any resistance to the new order was met with swift repercussions. Anyone who refused the chip was carted away to medical facilities across the country, locked down, and had the chip implanted by force. It was too risky. If the government discovered he was half-Platirian, he'd be locked away forever.

Cursing softly, he gripped the handles of his backpack. His BrainStaff was carefully tucked away inside. Over the years, he'd learned many tricks that had helped him survive living in a post-apocalyptic world. He felt its energizing glow as the officer advanced toward him. It was now or never.

Summoning its power, he teleported himself home. Looking around, he nearly panicked.

What the hell am I doing on the roof?!

He soon discovered the answer. Dozens of officers were swarming into his building, dragging people out of their homes and forcing them into unmarked cars.

The BrainStaff's power allowed him to peer through the roof. His condo had been vandalized. Documents, awards, and other sentimental items lay scattered across the floor. Food had been pulled from the fridge and trampled. He knew why. The serial numbers on the various packages and containers were registered to an unauthorized vendor.

A couple of years after President Musdin cheated his way into the Yellow House, Justin had connected with the resistance fighter. He sold food and ammunition to people who refused to bow down to the treasonous laws forced on them. Now his identity had been discovered.

Musdin's latest invention was a small microchip designed to go under the skin. It assisted COG, or Corporate Operation Genocide, in monitoring everyone's lives. It was a disgusting invasion of privacy. Those who opposed the procedure were eliminated or forced to work in labor camps.

He ducked when a bullet whizzed by his head. Several more bullets followed. Before he could think, a woman materialized out of thin air.

Silently, they assessed each other before she took out a sword and flew down to the officers. Without a word, she severed their limbs and heads. The sea of bullets failed to penetrate her armor.

I've seen that style of fighting before. But where? he thought.

Soon, she'd killed all of them without breaking a sweat. She took a moment to peruse the body parts and blood before looking up at him.

"Who are you?" he called down to her. "Where are you from? Is it Revani? Did my mother send you?"

She vanished as quickly as she had appeared.

"Follow her," he commanded the BrainStaff.

The chase was on. He flew through Space at a thousand miles a second, following the peculiar purple light trailing her.

He followed it until it crashed and bloomed inside a sparkling purple planet that seemed vaguely familiar to him. Not knowing how to break his fall, he plummeted into the warm purple grass and passed out.

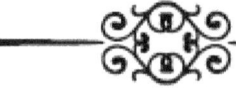

He awakened to find a crowd staring at him curiously. Sitting up, he clutched his aching head, shivering from the cool breeze. "Where am I?" he asked. "Where is this place?"

A female stepped forward. "This is JanIus." She inspected his clothes with a scanner. "Where did you come from?"

"I followed a purple light here. A female saved me—" He stopped abruptly. He didn't think it would be wise to let them know he was half-Human...or half-Platirian. "—so I followed her."

She looked him up and down. "Well, you shouldn't have."

The deep purple armor she wore looked sleek and light.

"We have strict laws on who enters our domain. Stand so you can be brought before our justice council," she said.

A male soldier grabbed his backpack. When Justin tried to snatch it out of his hands, the group of soldiers closed in to arrest him.

"That will be all, Captain Josin. I'll take it from here."

Captain Josin swiftly saluted the approaching figure. "A long life to our king!"

The crowd bowed to a young male dressed in purple armor. His café-au-lait complexion and periwinkle eyes would've surprised Justin had he not been acquainted with Alien aesthetics. Straw-colored, tightly coiled locks hung just past his shoulders. A highly polished gold and amethyst crown sat on his head.

Taking the backpack from Captain Josin, he looked around at the spectators and said, "I'm sure you all have better things to do than gawk at our new visitor, yes?"

Justin watched the crowd quickly disperse while the king peered inside the backpack. Suddenly, he sucked in a breath. Justin guessed he hadn't expected to see the head of a BrainStaff. He stared at Justin for several seconds before returning it to him.

"I'm King Leighton. I don't welcome strangers into my realm. It doesn't matter who you are or how you came here, I'd like for you to leave. Now."

Justin trained his eyes on a group standing outside an enormous medical chamber.

"Why do you have so many waiting to be seen?"

"I have far more Beings than skilled physicians to care for them all. Many of them have been dying off from common ailments, but without a competent workforce, my hands are tied."

"I'm Dr. Justin Ascencio. How about I stay and lighten the load? I don't plan to be here forever. Once I find the WomanForm who helped me and thank her, I'll leave quietly. There's no reason for anyone to suffer if they don't have to."

King Leighton nodded toward the backpack. "And what's to stop you from using that against me and taking over my realm?"

Justin hoisted it on his shoulder.

"I have no interest in ruling a planet. Things just got a little dangerous for me, so I need a place to hide. In my eyes, we'd be helping each other. I'd have a place to lay my head, and your subjects would have a competent professional to help them. I think it's a win-win for both of us."

King Leighton took in Justin's crisp, white shirt, black slacks, and expensive black loafers. "You have a BrainStaff but no armor. That means you're not a warrior, but I'm still not convinced you won't harm anyone."

Justin's lips curled upward. "I believe in saving lives, not ending them."

King Leighton paused for a moment, reflecting on his words. "All right, you have a deal. But I'll warn you, if anyone comes here causing trouble because of you, you'll have to go."

Justin extended his hand. "No problem, but I have a few requests, Your Highness."

King Leighton's grim expression hardened his handsome face. "What are they?"

"First, please call me Dr. Ascencio."

He watched the tension in the king's shoulders soften.

"All right," said King Leighton, shaking his hand. "What else do you need from me?"

Justin's lips curled upward. "All that flying made me hungry. I could use a good meal."

Fawn's Past

"WomenForms are incapable of being competent physicians. They're too emotional to keep a cool head when situations demand it. It's asinine to even think about."

Dr. Thom Azini took a gulp of coffee and wiped his mouth with an expensive, embroidered silk napkin. Once his practice became successful, he insisted on having his initials engraved on all of the linens.

His wife, Musha, darted a furtive glance between him and her daughter while nervously shifting the breakfast platters around on the table. She wouldn't challenge him. She never did. For once, Fawn wished her mother wasn't so meek and accommodating. What would it hurt to stand up to her husband and protect her daughter from his toxicity?

Steam rose from the eggs and freshly baked blueberry and lemon fritters. Usually, Fawn would've been overjoyed to eat one, but her father's words made the wad of sweetened dough and hot, spiced fruit feel like sandpaper in her mouth. She took a swig of milk, hoping it would make swallowing easier.

Fawn watched his mustache twitch. It always did whenever she displeased him.

"You want to deliver babies when your mind should be focused on bearing them."

His narrow gaze cut through her like a sword. "You have a perfectly decent MaleForm wanting to marry you, but you're treating him as if he's an insect slithering across the floor! When will you learn MaleForms exist to provide for WomenForms—not the other way around!"

He cast a suspicious glance at Musha. "I don't know who's been putting this foolishness in your head, but it needs to stop. Today. I don't want to hear any more about you wanting to be a doctor."

He helped himself to another fritter.

"It's required for every ChildForm to finish sixteen years of education. Your mother and I have faithfully abided by the law, and you'll finish your studies next month. I don't know why you're not satisfied with that. Most WomenForms marry right after they receive their certificate of completion."

Taking another sip of the fragrant, steaming coffee, he said, "Unmarried WomenForms end up alone and unwanted with nothing but space cats to talk to. Is that the kind of life you want for yourself?"

Fawn kept her eyes on her plate. To express how she felt would only make him angrier. She wasn't in the mood to have another argument her mother wouldn't help her win.

"I asked a question, Fawn," he insisted.

"May I be excused?" Fawn asked quietly.

"Oh, honey, you should finish your breakfast before you—"

Still glaring at Fawn, he said, "Be quiet, Musha."

Musha immediately fell silent.

"So you want to get up and leave while I'm trying to talk some sense into you? Are you appreciative of the life my career has provided you, Fawn? Had you been a MaleForm, I'd be the first to discuss plans for you to follow in my footsteps, but you're not!"

He wiped his mouth with the napkin again and threw it down on the table. Musha hastily replaced it with a clean one. He hated reusing things he thought were soiled.

"WomenForms aren't mentally competent to study the complexities of the brain or anything else outside of household responsibilities! You've been influenced by stories of that tyrant Revari and her wacky sister, Vivant. Years ago, she was seeing visions of her dead daughters, now she's ruling Platirius when she should've been thrown out on her ass by the justice council!"

A staunch misogynist, he refused to call the queens by their titles.

"But of course they won't do that, because they're all females too! In my grandfather's time, Platirius's justice council was run by MaleForms, and that's the way it should be today!"

Fawn watched the steam rising from the eggs, wishing she, too, could drift away.

"Chief Counselor Garoni's soul isn't at peace knowing his great-granddaughter, Adoni, is now leading the council. Not to mention that crazy Aiki who handed Old Kikhani to Revari on a silver platter. Revari is so arrogant, she named it after herself!"

His soaring temper made Musha's fingers tighten on her cup.

"How many MaleForms did she kill before Revari finally put her out of her misery? And that was after Revari killed King Hitam—who hadn't been seen in the galaxy since he left Aiki's worthless mother."

A vein throbbed furiously above his right eye. "He was minding his own business when they hunted him down and murdered him! Revari should be sentenced to death for what she did!"

He stopped ranting just long enough for Musha to refill his cup. "Revari murdered him in cold blood and stole his planet! It was easy for her—the little psychopath!"

He's so angry, he's resorted to using human words, thought Fawn.

"She killed her *own* father, throwing Platirius into chaos by splitting it in half. Never in history has a planet split." He pointed a finger in Fawn's face. "Never! And we all know how it rejoined, don't we? They killed off King Dimaro too—the last of the MaleForms in the Amorous family. He clawed his way out of a DeathCraft, and brought prosperity to Pletz, only to be put down like a dog by Vivant. I can't think of a more dishonorable way for a king to die!"

Against her better judgment, Fawn sighed. "No, Father. Platirius rejoined because Queen Vivant put her life on the line to keep Earth from being absorbed into it. The One intervened on her behalf for her bravery."

He set his coffee cup down with a sharp *clink*. "Bravery? Just what do you think is brave about that crazy whore? Are you trying to correct me, Fawn? The One doesn't help insane WomenForms advance over MaleForms."

He pointed at her and Musha. "You get this straight," he said through clenched teeth. "The One made *you* to submit to *us*!

Vivant stole Platirius from King Dimaro as sure as I'm sitting here. It's the only reason she's running it now!"

His steely glare traveled from Musha to Fawn. "That's what happens when you allow WomenForms to run amok. They destroy everything in their paths, inspiring others to get asinine ideas!"

His dull gray eyes bore into Fawn. "If you think you'll shame me with this idiotic notion of *independence*, you'd better think again. I've worked too long and too hard to build my practice into what it is today."

He drained the coffee cup and angrily pushed the dirty dishes toward Musha. "I won't have Beings whispering about my daughter wanting to go off half-cocked instead of knowing her place. You listen to me and you listen well, Fawn. This isn't Platirius or Old Kikhani!"

Revani, thought Fawn.

"This is JanIus, and here we do things the right way! We might be under a soft king, but his FatherForm believed in putting WomenForms right where they belong—beneath us!"

Musha blinked back tears as his tirade continued.

"I don't care what happens around the galaxy, you'll do what the WomenForms in my family have always done—get married and raise a family! I'm not listening to any more of this nonsense about you becoming a doctor. Is that clear?"

Fawn kept her eyes on her plate. "Yes, Father."

"Finish your breakfast and be on your way. Reports of Excellence are coming out today. I expect no less than perfection from you. May The One help you if you shame me."

Fawn nodded. The discussion had finally ended. He was set in his ways—nothing she said would change him. Musha hurried to clear the table and place the dishes in the sanitizer.

He looked at his watch. "I have to go. There's an outbreak going on. I need to get a handle on it before it gets out of control. I'm supposed to get new assistants in today, but I won't hold my breath."

He observed Musha expertly balancing the dishes with one hand. "I expect beef for supper tonight. You've been preparing far too many fowls this week. I work hard to provide for this family. The least you could do is act like it."

He never praised her or Fawn. He enjoyed laying down his never-ending list of demands, expecting them to be followed without question. Her appetite spent, she watched him leave without so much as a goodbye to his family. A spark of anger surged while her mother packed a few of the blueberry-lemon fritters in her lunch bag.

"These are so good," said Musha nervously. "It wouldn't hurt to take a few to your friends."

I don't have friends because everyone despises your husband.

"I made a nice turkey sandwich and fresh fried chips for your lunch today. I swear, Fawn, you're getting so thin. You should eat more. No MaleForm wants a WomanForm without a little meat on her bones."

Fawn's mouth curved slightly. She knew just how to get under her mother's skin. "You mean like General Legend of the Revaltians? Have you seen her curves? If I looked like that, I'd be in Heaven."

Musha frowned. "I wasn't referring to her, nor should you mention her in front of your father." She lowered her voice to a whisper. "He says she has the body of whore!"

"Why? Because she's well-endowed and has hips blessed directly by The One?"

Musha visibly paled as if she'd just fallen ill. "Fawn, please," she begged.

"He gripes about her, but he can't take his eyes off her," quipped Fawn. "I call hypocrisy."

"Fawn! That's enough! What your father says is right. You shouldn't idolize someone like that. She joined in helping a royal MaleForm get killed on Platirius!"

"He knew the rules, Mother. He chose to break them. No one forced him to."

"I heard she did. I heard she enchanted him with one of her spells."

Fawn knew exactly where she'd heard it from—her father. He used the same excuse whenever he was caught cheating on her mother. And Musha believed it every time.

"She's a general, Mother. Not a magician. And she's naturally beautiful. She doesn't need to trick a male to be with her."

Musha shook her head. "Fawn, I don't know what's gotten into you lately. Your father has provided us with a good life. Do you not understand how fortunate you are to live in a fine home with plenty of food to eat? We don't want for anything!"

Except love, thought Fawn.

"Go on," said Musha, handing her lunch bag to her. "You don't want to be late for classes."

Her anger at her parents hadn't subsided since she'd left the house. She knew why her mother wouldn't stand up to her father—she'd grown up in poverty. Her father never let her forget that he'd found her working in a dining chamber and had elevated her status to that of a physician's wife.

On numerous occasions, he had threatened to divorce her, but Fawn knew he wouldn't.

His reputation in the community was too important to him to shed the illusion of a devoted leader of his family. Not to mention times had changed. WomenForms had watched Queen Vivant and Queen Revari take thrones that had been reserved for MaleForms.

Despite doubts from the SexForms, each had successfully ruled their realms, including appointing female members to sit on justice councils and advocate for female rights.

After millions of years of oppression and misogyny, the female members of the royal Amorous family had changed the way most WomenForms thought of themselves and their places in society. They were done with having no options except becoming unemployed mothers with no ambition to call their own. It was the dawn of a new reckoning. They wanted more for themselves.

Cognizant that it wouldn't be easy for him to find another meek soul to take his verbal and physical abuse without consequences, he focused on breaking his wife's spirit. He'd spent years mentally beating down Musha long before he started hitting her.

Her earliest memories included Musha's stifled screams echoing through the walls of their luxurious home. She was seven summers the first time she witnessed him hitting her mother.

Dr. Azini stared down at his daughter before removing his foot from the back of his wife's head. She'd made the mistake of not putting enough butter in the mashed potatoes, causing him to throw a fit and send the bowl flying across the dining chamber.

The clumps of white vegetables were still hot when he pushed her face into them, holding her down with his foot. He waited until Fawn entered her advanced ChildForm years before taking a strap to her for the slightest mistakes.

Over the years, she'd come to realize her father enjoyed beating down the females in his family—with his words and his fists. As long as he could hide their bruises, he'd continue.

He enjoyed beating them on the last day of the week. He hadn't hit her for trying to reason with him—he couldn't excuse her missing classes until the bruises healed. He was extremely methodical. But Fawn knew at some point he'd nip her tiny spark of defiance in the bud.

He'd wait until the week ended before he'd begin shoving and hitting her where the bruises wouldn't show. Although she hated him for forcing his brutality on them, she hated her mother more for not opposing it.

She looked forward to graduating and moving out of her parents' home—but Fredi McCulloh wasn't an option. Once she escaped from beneath her father's tyrannical thumb, no MaleForm would ever have the power to control what she did and where she went. She'd make sure of it.

After sampling a few tasty dishes in the dining chamber, Justin was enjoying the tour of JanIus.

"I've only recently inherited the throne from my father," said King Leighton. "JanIus isn't as bad as Old Platirius was, but it still isn't as progressive as I'd like it to be. We still have far too many MaleForms who believe in the old system—keeping their feet on the necks of WomenForms."

The king sighed, shaking his head. "The complaints the MaleForms bring to the justice council are ridiculous. I recently appointed a WomanForm and am looking to add another. She's been very efficient at quelling the squabbles."

Slamming a fist into his palm, he said, "She's tough but fair, and that's exactly what we need. I admit that I have to check my own biases at times. Accepting change is hard, but we're still more intelligent than Humans."

The slight didn't offend Justin. His first trip to Space had made him view things differently after he returned to Earth.

"Earth is a firestorm right now," said Justin. "There are very few places where women are considered leaders. Some countries haven't elected a female president yet, so I totally understand."

King Leighton glanced at him out of the corner of his eye. "You're very knowledgeable about Humans. You must watch them a lot on the TranScreen."

Justin hid a smile.

If only you knew.

King Leighton pointed to a large, handsome building with a scalloped roof and beautiful, dark purple vines growing on the crystallized, lavender walls.

"That's the instruction chamber for our older ChildForms over there. And this," he said, stopping in front of a massive structure with large violet and lavender stained-glass windows, "is our largest medical chamber. We have around seven scattered about, but this is our newest model. Its equipment is far more advanced than the others."

The door opened when King Leighton scanned his hand across the TeleShield. "It's powered by the sun's rays during the day and the moon's energy throughout the night. Mind you, the ones on Platirius and Revani are far more extravagant, but I'm very proud of it."

Justin eyed the large, picturesque chamber and smiled. He couldn't wait to see the inside of it.

"I can feel your anticipation," said King Leighton. "Let's go inside, shall we?"

"After you, Your Highness," said Justin happily.

Chapter 2

He followed King Leighton, staring at the impressive machines in amazement. JanIus may have been smaller than other planets, but it was far from shabby. He saw foreign buttons, gadgets, and knobs he was eager to get his hands on.

Twenty-five rooms were completely furnished with two large TranScreens, a desk with an oversized, comfortable chair, two chrome examination tables, and sturdy chrome and crystal cabinets that held an abundance of medical supplies and equipment.

"All of our records are electronic. The doctors access the patients' medical history and transmit orders on their palms."

Justin feigned being surprised. "How is all of this funded?"

"We've been a peaceful race since my great-great-grandfather was on the throne. Avoiding wars has kept our lines of trade open with other realms."

Watching the JanIans go about their day made the king smile. "Our imported goods have never been taxed. I'm quite proud of that."

Justin thought of the tariffs they'd been subjected to. Nearly everyone he knew had lost everything they owned.

"The One has blessed us in keeping our economy stimulated without interruption. We're a tiny speck in the galaxy, but my Beings have plenty to eat and, until a few years ago, excellent medical care."

"What happened to your medical staff?" asked Justin.

"They were enticed by Queen Vivant's offer to join Platirius. As you know, before she signed her decree into law, MaleForms weren't welcome there. Many of our WomenForms aren't interested in marrying and they wanted wives."

A pretty JanIan caught Justin's eye. When she looked at him and frowned, he chuckled.

Some things never change, he thought.

"Queen Vivant heavily vetted them and weeded out all that held misogynistic views, so that's what JanIus was left with—the ones who don't believe WomenForms should advance. I'm down to one physician, and although he's skilled, his hatred of them has turned many of the female patients away."

The king nodded to the young female and was met with a bow and a smile before she hurried off.

"Likewise, no female physicians want to join my staff to treat MaleForms who believe they're inferior." He sighed. "So, I'm left with a conundrum. I need a male physician who will treat both SexForms with respect."

"I'm available if you'll have me," said Justin. "I don't get off on disrespecting females, nor will I co-sign the nonsense of your MaleForm subjects. If they don't like my views, they can continue seeing your other physician."

"Dr. Azini," said King Leighton. "That's a bargain. I need another skilled professional, so I can't turn you down, Dr. Ascencio."

They reached an exquisitely designed cottage a few yards from the main medical chamber. Justin was impressed by the breathtaking flower and herb gardens, as well as the ocean view.

"Thanks to the skills of a newly hired, young gardener, this is the nicest cottage on the lot," said King Leighton. "It has two bed chambers, two bath chambers, a private dining chamber that's attached to the living chamber, a library, and a recreation chamber. It's yours if you want it."

Justin couldn't believe his good fortune.

"It's a dream, but I can't imagine the cost to upkeep it."

"The rental fees are taken out of your pay each month. If you need a TravelCraft to get to other planets, I'll have one assigned to you for another small usage fee. You won't miss the fees. I pay my professional staff quite well. We don't need TravelCrafts to get around locally. Our environment is much cleaner than Earth's since we don't engage in polluting our air or water."

"You say the cottage has a dining chamber. Where would I purchase food?"

"You don't. Food deliveries are made every week. There's a panel located in all the cottages. After your order is placed, the supplies are delivered to your door from the gardening and processing chambers at no cost. No one on JanIus has ever paid for food and never will. Taxes cover medical expenses and funding for our instruction chambers."

"I assume the processing chamber handles meat?"

"Meat?" asked King Leighton.

"Yes, beef, chicken, turkey."

"Ah, did you learn that from the Human shows? Meat. What an interesting word."

"Well, what do you call it here?"

King Leighton grinned at him. "Beef, chicken, turkey."

He and Justin shared a laugh.

"Fair enough," said Justin. "I think I'll like it here."

King Leighton's vibrant eyes shone. "I hope you do, Dr. Ascencio," he said. "I sincerely hope you do."

J ustin worked quickly to attend to the needs of the JanIans. To his surprise, the WomenForms were so relieved to have a new physician that they flocked to him. He worked well into the night before the long list of patients had finally dwindled to two.

After prescribing medication to assist a WomanForm with stomach issues, the last name on the roster caught him by surprise.

"Gallium? What are you doing here? Did my mother send you to spy on me?"

Gallium smiled wryly. "It's been years since you've been gone, but you still think you're the main attraction, eh? I came to do landscaping work for King Leighton." Gallium's eyes traveled over the expansive examination room before settling on Justin's face. "Not that it's any of your business, Your Highness."

"Your brother is a doctor, but you're standing here in front of me. Do you really expect me to believe you need medical care?"

Gallium cocked his head. "I didn't bring him with me on my back, nor do I care what you believe."

"Where's Dr. Barrios?"

"Dead," he said flatly. He ignored Justin's stunned reaction.

"I'm sorry to hear that. I know how close you were. Does my mother know I'm here? What happened to him, if I may ask?"

"Ask away, but I'm not obligated to answer your questions. I'm not here to satisfy your curiosity, Prince Justin. As for Queen Revari, what goes on between you and your mother is your business. Please leave me out of it."

Justin wasn't convinced. "The BrainStaff I got when she took over Kikhani. It links us, doesn't it?"

Transfixed by the strange colors swirling in Gallium's eyes, Justin felt something he couldn't describe. He knew Gallium was an Alien, but he felt there was something more to him—something his mind couldn't quite grasp.

Gallium's deep baritone brought him out of the strange reverie. "I've never liked repeating myself, so I won't start now. I'm here for a bandage. May I have one please?"

Justin looked at the large cut on his arm. "Perhaps you should let me take a look at that."

Gallium smirked. "I'm a fast healer."

After receiving the bandage, Gallium carefully opened it and placed it on the cut.

"JanIus is a beautiful place, but there's very little vegetation outside of fruits and vegetables. The king wants me to correct it, so here I am. Some of us weren't lucky enough to be born into royalty."

The haughty gaze he cast Justin's way made him look more like a king than a gardener. "Not everything is about you."

Without another word, Gallium turned and walked away. More than a few of the WomenForms stopped to stare at him. A spark of jealousy flickered in Justin. He knew he was attractive, but Gallium's aesthetics outshone his by a mile.

"I don't know where I stand with that guy," muttered Justin.

After finishing up for the evening, he called the cleaning staff to sanitize and prepare the rooms for the next day. King Leighton forbade anyone from working over twelve hours a day. Any emergencies that happened after hours were shipped to neighboring planets.

Justin knew he was competent, but JanIus had been without a fully functioning medical staff for years. It wouldn't take long before he wore himself down—that wasn't good for the patients. Being a hybrid gave him an advantage. He understood the complexities of the anatomy of LifeForms outside of Earth. Yet, it wasn't enough.

He needed help. But from whom? He refused to ask Queen Revari. He knew she'd help him, but he wasn't ready to see her. So, who could provide what he needed? The answer materialized, but he didn't want to cause trouble for her. Still...something had to be done. And fast.

He expelled a frustrated breath. "Screw it. I won't know unless I ask."

Taking out his TeleScreen, he called the one Being he hoped could help him.

"Geneneral Legend speaking."

The face on the screen made her sit upright.

"Justin! You finally realize I still exist? Why did you stop talking to me? I haven't done anything to deserve that!"

He sighed. "I didn't want to deal with my mother."

"I see. And what does that have to do with me?"

"Well, you're her general aren't you?" he sneered. "Don't you have to do everything she tells you to?"

Her golden eyes flashed with fire. "Don't you dare take that tone with me. Keep in mind I'm still your aunt. I won't hesitate to straighten you out, *Dr. Ascencio*. I've earned my place as general many times over."

His fond memories of her instantly made him contrite.

She pointed at his face. "I've always been there for you, so don't go acting high and mighty with me. You got it?"

He had the nerve to look sheepish. "I'm sorry, Aunt Legend. You're right. I have no right to take my frustration out on you."

She nodded. "That's better. Have you come back to reunite with Queen Revari?"

"No, not really. I'm on JanIus."

Her curiosity piqued, she unconsciously leaned forward. "Why?"

He absently pivoted in the swivel chair. "It's a long story. Listen, I need your help."

Her hand rose in the air. "Oh? You haven't spoken to me in years, but now you need something? Why should I help you?"

"You know, you and Gallium speak very similarly. Very sharp and cutting."

She folded her arms across her breasts. "We're Coldarians. It comes with the territory. What do you need from me?"

"Medical staff. The WomenForms need more invasive procedures. I'm not a ParaNurture physician, I'm a brain surgeon. But I can still practice general medicine. A few of the females are pregnant, and many of them desperately need pelvic exams."

She leaned back in her chair. "Then send them out to other planets."

"I could, but I think it would be more convenient if they could have all of their needs taken care of here. Surely between Revani and Platirius you have enough to spare."

Her lips pursed. "We do, but you know that call would have to come from your mother and Queen Vivant. I don't have the authority to dispatch anyone to other realms except soldiers."

Cupping her face in her hands, she said, "But you knew that already. Your mother and aunt control the largest realms in the galaxy. Everything goes through them. And just how do you think you'll get staff from Platirius? Queen Revari hasn't spoken to Queen Vivant since we helped her defeat Prince Dimaro."

"Has Queen Vivant reached out to her?"

"Many times, but Queen Revari refuses to speak with her. She's never respected your mother's wishes to be left alone and never will. She keeps going on and on about transmitting photos of their mother. I know it's just a trick to make her talk to her."

"It may be, but I know my mother would want the photos. Do you think she'll give them to me?"

"No, but even if she did, what would you do with them, trade them for medical staff?"

He blessed her with a carbon copy of his mother's smile. "Exactly. Queen Revari gets the photos, Queen Vivant will get a false hope that she'll start talking to her again, and I'll get what I need. It's a win for everyone."

"If you think it'll be that easy, I've got news for you. Queen Revari can hold a grudge longer than most. It seems you inherited that from her. I'd be careful of Queen Vivant if I were you."

She took a sip of sweet PotterBerry juice. "She's not as nice as some would like to believe. When she lends a hand, there's always something in it for her. I doubt she'll transmit the photos just like that."

Justin rubbed a hand over his five o'clock shadow. "We'll see. I won't know until I try."

"Let me know how it goes. If she won't send any medical staff, you can count on Revani. Your mother wants you to have a good life despite what you may think of her."

He looked up at the stars and frowned. "I'm not ready to talk to her. Honestly, I don't know if I'll ever be."

A few seconds passed between them.

"Well, you know where to find her when you do. I wouldn't make her wait too long. She's mourned you for nearly all of your life. It's not fair to make her suffer more than she already has."

A large star shot across Space. "I'll keep that in mind. I love you, Aunt Legend."

"I love you too, Prince Justin."

Queen Vivant opened her TeleScreen and paused. "I must say, you're the last Being I expected to see."

"It's been a while. I understand you have some photos for my mother."

Her eyebrow raised. "I do, but what does that have to do with you?"

"I was wondering if you could send them to me and I'll make sure she receives them."

Queen Vivant laid aside the book she was reading. "Are you and she on good terms now?"

He shook his head. "No, but I feel she should have them. Gallium says she looks like my grandmother, but she doesn't know what she looks like."

"She's seen our mother's face, just not hers."

"Queen Opal," he said.

"Yes. Queen Revari never knew they were twins."

She drummed her silver nails on her desk. "I was hoping to reconnect with my sister. I don't see how transmitting the photos to you would make that a reality."

"Do you think it's right to dangle her mother over her head to force her to talk to you?"

Her silver eyes narrowed. "I don't think you have room to judge my actions. Not after what you did to me."

Unaware she was biting her lip until she tasted blood, she flicked the tip of her tongue over the stinging bit of flesh.

"You took General Legend's version of the truth and ran with it. There's nothing nefarious about wanting to see my sister."

He felt his blood pressure rising. "Which one? The general is your sister too, you know."

Her frosty smile matched her eyes. "You mean my father's alleged bastard? She'll never be acknowledged as royalty, so don't hold your breath."

He leaned forward. *There he is. Hello, King Dubian.*

"You know, I'll never understand why people believe my mother is the evil sister when clearly you are. Are you going to send the photos to me?"

"You're welcome to think what you please, and no, I will not. They don't belong to you. I'm willing to meet with Revari to peruse them and answer any questions she may have about our mother. If she wishes to share them with you, that's fine with me. But...I hear that's not all you need, nephew."

His look of surprise earned a smile from her.

"Word travels fast around the galaxy. Nothing gets by me...or your mother. You had to know we knew you were here. If not, you're extremely naïve...or as arrogant as my father."

"It's odd you should say that, considering your arrogance is directly responsible for my father's death. Let's not having a pissing contest about that, alright?"

She ignored his imperious tone.

"If you need medical staff, you may have them. I'm shipping out two hundred and fifty qualified professionals tomorrow. I'm sure Revari will double that amount. Does King Leighton have enough room for them to live comfortably?"

His mouth opened. "Uh...yes he does."

"What is it? You didn't expect me to help you?"

"Not really."

She sucked her teeth. "You've never tried to get to know me. You came to Platirius judging me due to mistakes I made in my past. I've paid for them many times over. You don't know how many times I wake up and see your father's face."

Her grip tightened on the TeleScreen. "It's disconcerting to look at you now—you bear a strong resemblance to him. It took a long while to forgive you for what you did, but even I had to admit I deserved it."

She looked up at a painting of her holding an infant Queen Revari. King Carlomon had it commissioned shortly before they were stolen from his palace.

"Had your parents been left alone, I have no idea how long your father would've lived or if she would've returned to Platirius with you after he passed. I had no right to interfere in her life. Despite what you think, I haven't been able to forgive myself for that."

"So you're providing the staff out of guilt?"

She cocked her head. "I'm helping you because you're my sister's ChildForm. You could've turned out to follow in my father's footsteps, but you didn't. Instead of hurting Beings, you want to heal them. I admire that about you. I hope, in time, we'll learn to treat each other as proper family."

"I can't make any promises, but I appreciate the help. I hope you'll change your mind about the photos. Give her the respect you didn't show her when she was carrying me. Allow her to decide when she wants to see you. From what I've heard about him, the two of you have a lot more of your father's ways than you think."

Queen Vivant sighed. "Good night, Prince Justin. I'll dispatch the staff in the morning."

"Thank you, Queen Vivant."

"You're welcome," she said.

He disconnected the transmission and sighed. It had been a long day.

Fawn's Past

Fawn stifled a yawn as the day drew to a close. She was tired and restless. She hadn't slept well the night before after listening to her mother pleading with her father to stop hitting her. He always went several days with pseudo shows of affection before he started up with the violence. She'd be able to sleep tonight.

Mrs. Corral stood at the front of the classroom, signaling for the students to be quiet.

"This is the final week before graduation. I've already transmitted your Reports of Excellence. I want to inform you about a new program introduced by Queen Revari and Queen Vivant for students interested in majoring in Medical Studies."

She clapped her hands together excitedly. "They're willing to sponsor over one thousand female students, providing a free education for those who wish to become ParaNurture physicians."

Fawn's fatigue instantly vanished. She sat up straight, focusing keenly on Mrs. Corral.

"This program isn't for the faint of heart. It will take intense years of study—though not as long as it takes for the idiotic Humans to become physicians."

Mrs. Corral waved her hand. "But I digress. The training is on Platirius and Revani. Afterward, you'll be assigned across the galaxy to set up your practices. I have sign-up sheets available for anyone who is interested. Please see me after I dismiss you."

Fawn bit her nails with anticipation. If she were accepted into the program, she'd be safe from her father. He wouldn't dare cross either of the queens. Impatiently, she shuffled her feet until the last student left. Only a handful a female students remained seated.

"Are all of you interested in the sponsorship? Very good! Please have your ParentForms complete the forms I'm transmitting and return them to me tomorrow."

Fawn groaned inwardly. There was no way they'd agree to her enrolling in the program. She raised her hand.

"Mrs. Corral, I'm nineteen summers now. Do my ParentForms still have to sign off?"

"Well...no...but I'm afraid you'll need someone to vouch for you, Fawn. It could be any AdultForm in good standing in the community—it doesn't have to be your ParentForms."

Fawn lowered her head. Mrs. Corral held up her palm to transfer the documents to her.

"Take the application. I'm sure you'll find someone who can provide a proper recommendation. Aren't you friends with

Princess Tarah? If Queen Vivant vouches for you, you're as good as accepted."

Fawn bit her lip. Dare she ask her?

Mrs. Corral seemed to read her mind. "You won't know until you ask. If I were you, I wouldn't mention the program to your father. He won't hear anything from me."

For a brief moment, disgust overshadowed Mrs. Corral's serene nature. For the first time, Fawn realized the instructor hated her father. He might have thought he was a pillar of the community, but most of JanIus's WomenForms didn't agree.

On more than a few occasions, they'd noted the bruises she and her mother had desperately tried to hide and how slowly they moved and sat after one of his violent outbursts. Dr. Azini was revered only in his mind and by the MaleForms who emulated his despicable behavior.

Fawn nodded, scanning the terms of the contract before she closed her hand. Once Beings reached nineteen summers, they were able to send and transmit documents without their ParentForms' knowledge or approval.

However, if they still lived within the family dwelling, getting permission to leave JanIus was mandatory. Mrs. Corral stopped her at the door.

"Fawn, this sponsorship may prove to be very beneficial for you. Not just in furthering your education, but ensuring you receive what's coming to you when your father passes. Queen Revari is notorious for putting bad fathers in their places. If you impress her, you just might get everything you want."

Imagining her father inside a DeathCraft didn't bother her at all.

"If she selects you, do your very best to please her. Despite what Beings think about her, she and Queen Vivant believe in the advancement of WomenForms."

Mrs. Corral rummaged inside her oversized bag. "I'm glad I recommended you as a peer mentor to Princess Tarah. I suspect it will work in your favor. The princess holds you in high regard, and that goes a long way with Queen Vivant. I think the time has come to reap the benefits."

"Thank you, Mrs. Corral. I'll ask Princess Tarah if Queen Vivant can recommend me before he returns from his conference."

"That's next week," said Mrs. Corral, pulling out her TeleScreen. "Ask her now. Before you go home."

She handed Fawn the TeleScreen. Princess Tarah answered almost immediately.

"Hi, Fawn! This is a surprise. We don't get together until the end of the week. Is something wrong?"

"Hello, Your Highness," said Fawn shyly. "No, nothing is wrong."

Princess Tarah frowned. "It's been three years. When are you going to stop addressing me so formally? Just call me Tarah."

"I've tried, Your Highness, but I can't." She lowered her head.

"Please raise your head and look at me," commanded Princess Tarah. "You're not just a tutor, you're my friend. I hope the feeling is mutual."

Fawn kept her head down, too shy to speak.

Princess Tarah sighed. "Maybe one day you'll abide by my wishes. Are you calling to cancel our tutoring session?"

"Oh no! Nothing like that! It's just...well...it's about the ParaNurture physician program."

Princess Tarah stirred the ice in her drink. "Yes, I heard about that."

She stopped stirring and looked up, her eyes wide with excitement. "Are you applying for it? I know how long you've wanted to be a doctor. By The One, Fawn! This could be your chance!"

Fawn nervously bit her lip. "My parents will never agree to it. I was wondering if...well... Do you think Queen Vivant will provide a recommendation for me?"

"Hold on," said Princess Tarah.

She turned to a tall figure Fawn couldn't see.

"Mother, my friend would like to apply for your and Aunt Reve's ParaNurture program. She's an exceptional student. Will you advocate for her? She needs a letter of recommendation to submit with her application."

Fawn's eyes grew wide when the queen sat next to her daughter and peered into the TeleScreen. She held her breath when the queen's beautiful eyes roamed over her face. Although she'd tutored Princess Tarah for years, she'd never met her mother.

Queen Vivant's warm smile flowed over Fawn like sunshine. "Of course I will. Hold up your palm, Fawn."

Fawn did as she commanded. Before she knew it, a detailed letter was transmitted to her palm. In awe, Fawn traced Platirius's royal seal with the tip of her finger. Queen Vivant smiled at her daughter, pushing a lock of hair off her face.

"Is that all you needed, baby?"

"Yes, Mama, thank you for helping her."

Queen Vivant's gaze sought Fawn again, who was still speechless.

"Than-thank you, Your Majesty," she stammered.

"It's my pleasure, Fawn. Nothing makes me happier than seeing WomenForms follow their ambition."

She looked at Princess Tarah. "I have a meeting with the Vivacians. I'll see you later." Kissing the princess's forehead, she said, "In a while, daughter."

"In a while, Mother."

Princess Tarah turned back to Fawn. "See? Now all you have to do is complete the application and send it to Colonel Sheila. She's on the panel to review all the applicants. There's no way you won't get in!"

Tears filled Fawn's eyes. "I can't thank you enough, Princess Tarah. I'm so nervous!"

"Don't be. You'll make a great physician. And don't worry. You're number one in your class. I want to be the first to hear when you're selected. See you at the end of the week!"

"Of course!" said Fawn happily. "Thank you again."

"In a while," said Princess Tarah before disconnecting the call and sending another transmission.

Colonel Sheila's face appeared on the TeleScreen.

"Yes, Princess Tarah?"

"Mother just sent her recommendation. She should be sending the application soon."

"Fast work, Princess. I'll be on the lookout for it. Thank you. In a while."

"In a while."

Colonel Sheila looked up. "Everything is set in motion, Your Highness. The JanIan student is applying for your program."

Queen Revari's fiery red gaze glowed fiercely with anticipation.

Chapter 3

Justin woke up in a world of dazzling blue. A king sat at a large table, looking out the window at ChildForms playing in the snow. The king smiled and waved when they greeted him.

Justin heard a knock at the door. Without knowing who was behind it, he ran to the king and shouted, "No! Don't open the door! Wait! King Carlomon!"

He woke up panting hard.

King Carlomon? Where have I heard that name before? Gallium!

He remembered Gallium mentioning him on Revani, but he couldn't recall who he was. He'd been so angry with his mother that he'd tried to erase everything he'd experienced the last time he was in Space.

It had helped mask the pain for a while. Until he discovered the BrainStaff in his closet one morning. He had no idea he'd been given one when Queen Revari took over Kikhani. He guessed the ChildForms of royal figures received them by default.

Then why had she lied to him about how he could acquire one? What else had she lied to him about? There were many questions, but he didn't trust her to answer any of them.

Rubbing his hand over his eyes, he sat up, shielding them from the blinding sun. He looked at the fancy timekeeper built into the wall. It was time to get up and get ready for work. Wondering if Gallium was working at the palace, he made a mental note to swing by and see him on his lunch hour.

When he stepped into the shower, water cascaded down from the walls. There were no shower heads. He moaned when the hot stream hit his body. For him, everything was more innovative and convenient in Space.

He'd missed how things operated outside of Earth. Everything smelled and tasted better—he had no idea why he'd been taught it was superior to other planets. It wasn't.

His Aunt Legend had been right—Humans knew nothing about how life operated on other planets with different LifeForms. He found himself reluctantly agreeing with the Aliens that Earth was at the bottom of the galaxy's totem pole.

The eerie dream continued to plague him while he scrubbed his skin with the woodsy-scented soap and bathing cloth.

"Why am I dreaming about someone I've never seen before?" he asked aloud.

Fully intending to satisfy his curiosity, he prayed Gallium could assist him.

H is first patient was difficult to dismiss. Not because he didn't want to see her go. She was looking for a different kind of bedside manner.

"So you're telling me you've gone all this time looking that incredible without being married?" she asked.

"Er—yeah. Now, Ms. Dill, I've done a complete work-up, but I haven't been able to determine why you're experiencing pain in your thigh."

She fluttered her long eyelashes at him. "That's because you haven't massaged it properly."

His eyebrow rose. "Excuse me?"

"My thigh. You haven't given it a good massage. Once you do, you'll feel a spot that's very hot. Here," she said, taking his large hand in hers. "I'll show you."

She placed his hand high up on her hip and started moving it in wide circles. "See?" she purred. "Don't you feel...warmth?"

She moved his hand up to her belly and higher, to her breasts.

He snatched his hand away. "Ms. Dill, you said the pain was in your thigh, not your cleavage!"

She squinted at him suspiciously. "What's a cleavage?"

"Your..." He cleared his throat. "Your breasts."

"Oh." She clapped her hands gleefully. "That's Human lingo, right? You've been assigned to Earth to study them? We don't call them that here. Or breasts. Breasts belong on chickens."

Justin blinked once. She was the most peculiar female he'd ever met.

"These," she said, pointing to her chest, "are DingoPops."

"DingoPops?" he echoed in disbelief.

"Yes. What? You don't believe me? That's much better than cleavage." She wrinkled her nose. "Cleavage sounds like you're hacking something to death!"

He sighed heavily. "Okay. There's nothing wrong with your...DingoPops or your thigh. Actually, you're perfectly healthy."

She pouted. "Then why do I feel so hot? I need something to cool me off, Dr. Ascencio."

"Well, I can't help you with that. What you want is beyond my scope of job duties."

She frowned. "You're not going to get many dates if you keep talking like a Human!"

"Colorful communication keeps you young, Ms. Dill," he said smoothly. "Now, if you don't mind, I have other patients who *are* sick. Please take care of your bill at the front desk."

"Who would be proud of sounding like a Human?" she muttered, pulling her skirt down over her shapely thighs.

"Who would want to show their DingoPops to a stranger?" he tossed as he added up her bill and transmitted it to her.

A fierce scowl clouded her lovely face.

"That's not very polite," he said.

"Neither are you for turning me down. I'm a lot prettier than Human women!"

He flashed a charming smile. "Yes, you are, but I'm not looking for love. I'm here to help, not to take advantage of you."

It worked. She beamed at the compliment.

"Thank you for noticing!"

She hopped down off the examination table and straightened her clothes. "I'll be back when something's wrong," she tossed over her shoulder.

He chuckled. He thought women on Earth were something, but nothing had prepared him for some of the personalities of JanIus's WomenForms.

"Have a great day, Ms. Dill."

"You too, Dr. Ascencio!"

The next patients were three small male ChildForms.

"Triplets!" exclaimed Justin. "What a nice surprise!"

The trio looked up at him miserably. He smiled at the WomanForm standing next to them. "What seems to be the problem?"

Her black eyes seared into them like lasers. "They ate an entire case of chocolates! I was saving them to make fudge for a bake sale, but they ate it all! Now they're sick as space hounds, and I don't feel a bit sorry for them! But I'd be a poor excuse for a MotherForm if I didn't bring them here."

"An entire case of chocolates?"

"Yes," she said, clearly annoyed with their greed and his disbelief.

"That one," she said, pointing to a large crate sitting on the floor.

Baking Chocolate was spelled in gold letters on each side. The young ChildForms cast guilty looks at each other.

"Lord," he muttered. "How are you feeling, triplets? Does it hurt when I touch here?"

They groaned when he placed his hand on their round, extended bellies.

"The only way to make you feel better is to get it all out of your system. So I'm prescribing a laxative, and if that doesn't work fast enough, I'm sending you home with enemas too."

"Thank you, Dr. Ascencio," she said, placing the laxatives into her stylish bag.

"You can pick up the enemas at the checkout window just before you reach the main entrance."

Turning back to the triplets, he said, "Chocolates are delicious, but that doesn't mean you should eat a whole case! By the looks on your faces, I'm pretty sure you've figured out that wasn't the smartest thing to do, right? I don't think I need to warn you not to do it again."

"Oh, they will," she said. "This is the third time they've done it."

Justin looked from her to the three small, guilty faces.

"Then I suggest you keep it under lock and key," he said, peering up at their medical history on one of the TranScreens.

"It says here they're five."

"Yes, five summers. They're old enough to know better!" she snapped.

"If they've done it more than once, then clearly they don't know."

Shifting her reproachful gaze from the triplets, she sneered at Justin. "Are you calling me a bad ParentForm?"

Justin shook his head. "Not at all. I'm merely suggesting you should safeguard the sweets. It's okay to have a treat now and then, but overeating will only earn them another trip back here."

Still looking at their charts, he said, "I see they've been here a number of times for a host of things—sprained ankles, broken bones, various cuts and lacerations..."

He went silent as a sinking feeling formed in the pit of his stomach.

She harrumphed. "At least Dr. Azini would've given them a good smack upside their skulls!"

He looked up at her sharply. "I'm not Dr. Azini, nor would I ever raise my hand to my patients. Where is their FatherForm?"

She seemed taken aback by the question.

"He's in the military," she snapped. "He's often gone for long spans of time, leaving me here to raise his brats!"

"His brats?" he echoed.

Transferring his gaze to the ChildForms, he asked, "You aren't their biological MotherForm?"

"Of course not! No sons of mine would be so dumb!"

"I see," he said evenly. "Are you married to their FatherForm?"

She bristled at his cool tone. "Am I inside a medical chamber or in front of the justice council?"

"If I suspect you've been abusing them, that's exactly where you'll be," he promised.

"Are you out of your mind? You have no right to make such asinine accusations!"

Justin turned away from the TranScreen. "You may be their authority figure, but here, I make the rules."

Sensing the swift change in his mood, she hastened to make amends. "I—I meant no disrespect, Dr. Ascencio!"

"Leave," he said. "I want to talk to them alone."

"But I have to get them home for supper—"

He kept his tone low to avoid frightening the triplets. "I said get out. I've been briefed on the protocol for ChildForm abuse. Until I'm satisfied that they haven't been mistreated, they won't be going home with you. Don't make me ask you twice."

She scurried out of the examination chamber, leaving the frightened triplets behind. Realizing he towered above them at over six feet, he hooked his foot on a stool and pulled it over. The brothers watched him ease his athletic body down gently onto it.

"Okay, guys, what's going on with the chocolate, huh? Why are you eating so much of it?"

The triplet on the left quickly perked up. "Well, she—"

He stopped abruptly when the brother in the middle jabbed him in the side with his elbow.

Justin raised his hands. "Hold up, guys. This is a safe space, and we're all friends here. It's okay if you don't trust me well enough to say anything, but don't stop him from telling me what's going on. I'm here to help you."

The male in the middle furrowed his brow. "Father will get mad at us if he has to come home to stay," he said defiantly. "He has an important job in the military. We're gonna grow up to be just like him."

"Oh? What do you want to be when you grow up?" asked Justin.

He quickly clamped his mouth shut, refusing to say anymore.

Justin sighed and rubbed a hand over his mouth. His inexperience with ChildForms didn't deter him from trying to earn their trust.

"The amount of bruising I see around your heads isn't normal. Do you understand if someone doesn't stop giving you blows to the skull, you may not live to be your father's age?"

The ChildForms looked at each other incredulously.

"Is it true what she said? Does Dr. Azini hit you?"

"Only when we get out of line," said the brother sitting on the right. "My name is Tio." He pointed to the brother on the left, then to the one in the middle. "That's Tyer, and the one glaring at you is Tautumn."

"Dr. Azini's job is to help you feel better, not hurt you, whether you're in line or out of it. He's not your parent. Does your FatherForm hit you?"

Tio's eyes widened. "Oh, no. Never," he said.

48

"So your father is nice to you? What do you think he'd do to Dr. Azini if he knew he hit you?"

"He'd kill him," said Tyer without hesitation. "And our SecondMother too. He told us so. She kisses Dr. Azini sometimes when she thinks we're asleep."

Justin raised his eyebrow. "Dr. Azini comes to your home?"

"Only at night," admitted Tio.

Justin filed that bit of information away for later. "Does your SecondMother hit you?"

"Sure, all the time," said Tyer. "She says the only reason she married our father is for the military funding. She says if we die on her watch, she'll get the death funds for all of us—especially our father. Sometimes she gives him yucky green stuff to drink that she gets from Dr. Azini."

Encouraged by the compassion in Justin's eyes, Tyer continued. "It makes him so sick that he can't leave his bed to play with us when he's home. Then he goes back to work and he's all right again. We ate the chocolate because it was unopened."

Tautumn still hadn't said a word, but Tio said, "We're sorry, Dr. Ascencio. We didn't mean to eat it all. We were just so hungry!"

Justin's heart sank. *She's poisoning them, hoping they'll die.*

Unbeknownst to the ChildForms, he'd been recording everything they said on his palm.

He sighed again. "I can't let you go home with her, but don't worry. King Leighton is very kind. He has a wonderful system in

49

place for you to stay with a family who'll be nice to you until we can contact your father."

"But what about his job?" asked Tyer. "He can't be a soldier and stay home with us."

"All soldiers have paid leave. More than enough for him to find suitable arrangements for you to be properly cared for so that he can return. You don't have to live like this."

Tautumn's suspicious nature wasn't lost on Justin. "Why should we trust you? Dr. Azini can make us disappear and no one would find us. Who's going to stop him? You?"

What a spunky little tyke, thought Justin. "He's not going to make anyone disappear."

Justin could tell Tautumn hadn't believed a word he'd said. "He could hit you too."

Justin chuckled. "He's not crazy enough to hit me. I'm bigger and stronger than he is. Cowards like him target those who can't fight back. I doubt he's fought a MaleForm in his entire lifespan."

Tears smarted in Tio's eyes. "Where will we go?" he whispered.

"To a very fine family where you'll be well fed and cared for," said a voice. "I've dispatched your FatherForm to return to JanIus. He should be here within a two-day span."

They all turned to King Leighton, who nodded to Justin. He'd heard the transmission through his TeleScreen.

"You've done very well! I'm so happy to have such brave young MaleForms under my authority. Your FatherForm will be very proud of you."

He turned to the door. "Mr. and Mrs. Overmill? Would you step in here please?"

A young couple joined them. Justin spied the enemas in Mrs. Overmill's hands.

"I have these and the laxatives you prescribed, Dr. Ascencio. My husband and I were never blessed by The One to have ChildForms of our own, so we've opened our home to the triplets until a permanent solution can be arranged for them."

"Mr. and Mrs. Overmill are a blessing to us," said King Leighton. "They're just one of the families that step in to help when needed. Your father will retrieve you from their home once he returns. He has more than enough leave time to make arrangements for you."

Cautiously, the trio slid off the examination table. Mrs. Overmill leaned down to them. "Everything will be all right now, I promise."

They looked up at the tall form of Mr. Overmill, who smiled down at them.

"Oh, don't worry about him," said Mrs. Overmill. "He's a big, cuddly bear."

"Naomi and I would give anything to have fine sons like this," said Mr. Overmill. "I just don't understand what goes through the mind of Beings who take pleasure in hurting ChildForms. What do they get out of it?"

"Low self-esteem or the need for control. Who knows what goes on in the minds of abusers?" said Justin.

King Leighton nodded to the Overmills.

"Let us go," said Mrs. Overmill. "If you're all better in the morning, we'll have a fine breakfast. How does that sound?"

Tautumn observed the little round hat, fashionably tailored suit jacket, silk blouse, knee-length skirt, and medium heels in eye-catching shades of beige and cream. She had a pert nose, and her almond-shaped eyes were the color of warm honey.

"Are you a good cook?" he asked.

Her eyes sparkled mischievously. "Oh no, not me. But my husband makes the best waffles and fried ham and eggs on this side of the galaxy!"

The triplets' mouths dropped.

"I've never heard of a WomanForm who couldn't cook," muttered Tautumn.

She laughed. "Well, you have today, young Tautumn. We'll test his skills once we get you and your brothers up and running, alright?"

Tautumn looked over at Mr. Overmill, but didn't say anything. He didn't look very convinced. The couple took their small hands in theirs. Tautumn, staying close to Mrs. Overmill, looked back at Justin and followed them out.

Since his personality was more outgoing than his brothers, Justin suspected he'd received the worst of the beatings. Justin loathed Dr. Azini more for trying to suppress his natural spark.

"Without their testimony, I don't have enough to bring Dr. Azini in front of the justice council," confessed King Leighton. "I'm reluctant to put such young ChildForms in front of the justice counselors. It would help if someone in his household would testify against him. Then I could have him sentenced and locked away for good."

"Where's the SecondMother?"

"She's been arrested for contributing to the negligence of ChildForms. They'll never see her again. We can't have her charged with attempted murder until we find evidence she's been poisoning the family. To my knowledge, the father visited the medical chamber for an upset stomach on a few occasions, but we weren't able to name the substance found in his system."

King Leighton picked up an unopened package of gauze. "I don't know how he'll respond once he learns she tried to kill all of them, or of her affair with Dr. Azini. I dispatched a few of my soldiers to the family's home searching for the substance the triplets said she placed in their food."

Placing the gauze in one of the cabinets, he said, "If it's found, we can charge her. That alone will ensure she never sees the light outside of my confinement chamber again."

"That's where she belongs," said Justin. "What a detestable WomanForm."

"My staff had raised suspicions of her before Platirius opened its borders. After most of the medical staff left, the issue was dropped. Dr. Azini had full rein to do what he pleased—to her and the triplets."

The king's mouth twisted in disgust. "I've never liked him, but he's the only doctor we have. I had no idea what was going on until today."

He looked up at a corner. "I'm having my surveillance team install visual equipment throughout the medical chambers."

"If he knows he's being watched, I doubt he'll be stupid enough to get caught on camera," said Justin.

"That's the point. He'll be on his best behavior at work, and it'll keep the patients safer until I can nail him."

"Yes, but won't that make things harder for his family?"

"It might. None of the cottages are monitored, and I doubt everyone would agree to it. I don't want to infringe on anyone's personal privacy. Installing them inside the medical chambers were a last resort."

He sat across from Justin. "I thought long and hard about it, but it had to be done. If there are more like Dr. Azini, I want them out of my service chambers and locked away for the rest of their lifespans. I don't want innocent Beings to suffer."

"You say he lives with family?" asked Justin. "How many?"

"He has a wife and a daughter—Musha and Fawn. Very nice WomenForms. Fawn is completing her medical residency now. Have you met her?"

The news caught Justin off guard. Dr. Azini didn't seem to be the type who'd encourage his daughter to become a physician.

"No," said Justin. "I haven't had a chance to meet anyone outside of patients."

He missed a peculiar expression that flashed across King Leighton's face.

"Did Fawn have her father's blessing to continue her studies?"

"No," said King Leighton. "But he didn't have a choice."

The king's tone suggested he didn't want to discuss Dr. Azini anymore.

Looking at his watch, Justin said, "It's past my lunch hour. Do you mind if I take a walk on the palace grounds? There's someone I need to speak with."

King Leighton approached a miniature model of all the planets in the galaxy. Absently spinning Earth with the tip of his finger, he said, "Of course. You're free to go anywhere you please."

Without looking up at Justin, he asked, "Do you know Gallium? I saw you speaking with him the other day."

"Not really," said Justin.

It was true. Although he'd spent time with him on Revani, Gallium had kept most Beings at a distance—including Justin. He hadn't seen Gallium communicate with anyone except for Dr. Barrios, Queen Revari, and General Legend unless he had to.

Time and Dr. Barrios's death had widened the gulf between them. Justin sensed losing Coldarius and his family had been deeply traumatic for Gallium.

The king's hand closed over Earth. "I hope you don't think I'm being intrusive. I don't know much about anything beyond

JanIus. I've seen Beings live much longer when they keep their noses out of others' business."

The king's strange warning floated through Justin's mind as he strode out the doors into the crisp, clean air. Halting abruptly, he turned and stared at the enormous medical chamber. Without the sun's brightness, an ominous shadow was cast over the sparkling indigo lawn, making it look as if it were soaked with blood.

How did he know I wanted to see Gallium?

He decided to deal with it later—whatever "it" was. The need to solve the mystery surrounding King Carlomon was far more pressing. He quickened his pace to find Gallium.

G allium was kneeling on the ground, planting extraordinary purple roses outside a small jewelry shop.

"Still beautifying the place, huh?" asked Justin.

Gallium's hands were moving so fast, that Justin paused to stare at them.

"Do the questions ever cease, Prince Justin?"

"King Leighton must've told you I was coming."

"No. You did. I could feel your footsteps getting closer. Some of the plants protested when you stepped on them."

Frowning, Justin shot a glance over his shoulder. "I don't see any plants."

Gallium never took his eyes off the seedlings. "I'm speaking of the plants underground."

Justin looked down at the well-manicured lawn as if expecting to see a plant shoot out of it, before looking back at Gallium.

"You certainly are one of the strangest men I've ever met."

Gallium turned to look at him. "I'm no man."

The strange feeling Justin felt when they'd met the other day washed over him. Gallium's eyes changed from sea-green to an array of bright, blazing colors.

"Will you at least admit you're strange then?"

Gallium grunted. "Strange to a Human? That's the biggest laugh of my lifespan. If the galaxy measured life by the finite wisdom of the Human mind, we'd all be in trouble."

"Ah, but I'm half-MaleForm too," said Justin.

"Hm. I've only seen that side of you when you had King Dubian's BrainStaff."

"It's not something I want to hold again," said Justin solemnly. "It made me...crazy."

Gallium covered another bulb with dirt. "I'll be the first to admit you're right. For a while, I thought he'd returned from the grave."

Pausing to water the small mound of dirt, he said, "I don't think you should return to Platirius."

"That may be true, but I have questions only Queen Vivant can answer. And..." His voice trailed off.

Gallium's half-smile was pitying. "And you want to see General Lyric again."

He wondered if the prince knew his scowl was the perfect imitation of his mother's.

"I never mentioned her."

"You didn't have to. You're not the first MaleForm who's had his heart broken by a headstrong WomanForm," said Gallium, digging another hole in the ground. "And you won't be the last. Now, what do you want from me?"

Justin sucked his teeth. "Straight to the point as ever!"

"It's the only way I know how to be," said Gallium. "If you haven't noticed, I'm busy. I'd like to finish my work and return home. I promised my wife I'd return home on time for supper."

"Who wears the pants, you or Aunt Legend?"

Chuckling, Gallium wiped his hands on his trousers. "Are you always so rude?"

"Me? Rude? Gallium, your tongue is sharper than that gardening thing lying next to you."

Gallium picked up the blade and jabbed it down hard into ground. "That may be, but I don't ask questions that are none of my business."

"Then here's a question that's right up your ally. Who is King Carlomon? I dreamed about him last night."

Chapter 4

That caught Gallium's attention. His hand stopped just short of picking up another rose bulb. Seemingly unable to speak, an uncomfortable silence passed between them.

"I told you about him. He was your great-grandfather and Coldarius's last king."

Justin knelt down next to him. "In my dream, he was sitting in an expensive looking castle, in a...kitchen...although you call it a private dining chamber, when someone knocked at his door. Whomever was on the other side of it was awful. They wanted to hurt him. I tried to get him not to open the door, and then I woke up. What could that mean?"

Gallium stabbed at the soil again. "I have no idea." He turned to look at Justin. "It really doesn't matter, does it? He's been gone for a long time."

"Did you like him?"

"Of course I did. All of his subjects did. He was a good and decent MaleForm. His loss is still felt after all this time. What's all this about?"

Justin shook his head. "I wish I knew. But if King Dubian was once a part of me, wouldn't it be logical that King Carlomon's spirit lives in me too?"

Gallium finished planting the last of the roses. "Yes, it's possible. He's the other side of your mother's family." He stared off into the distance. "King Carlomon's power was absorbed into Platirius when Coldarius was conquered. When you held the BrainStaff, you were controlled by his spirit too, not just the evil kings."

"Then why didn't I hear his voice? Why were King Anemi and King Dubian so desperate to control me?"

Gallium rose to his feet. "They wanted you to take Platirius's throne. And they still do."

He wiped the back of the blade against his dirt-streaked trousers. "I don't know why you're being plagued by dreams of King Carlomon. Coldarius is gone—it has no throne for you to inherit. Maybe he's trying to tell you something, but I'm not a sorcerer. Maybe Jia, Cyen, or Cita can help you."

"I don't want help from the Revaltians."

"Then why do you want mine?" asked Gallium. "Why bring up painful memories I've buried like these flowers?"

"I don't mean to make your life difficult, Gallium. I just want to know where I come from. You told my mother about Coldarius."

"Yes, but you're not her. I'm under no obligation to tell you anything."

"But you have obligations to her?"

Gallium nodded once. "Of course. I promised Queen Dellah I'd watch after and protect Queen Revari until I died, and that's what I intend to do. That means protecting her from all harm—including you."

Justin felt his temper slipping. "What's with all the hostility, Gallium? You treated me well when we were on Revani."

"That was before you broke your mother's heart. I have no use for anyone who hurts her."

"What's your deal? Are you her lover too?"

"You're just as stupid as a red sun," snapped Gallium. "You get this straight. I was there the day she was born. And I've been in love with General Legend since long before you were alive. Only a fool would think a love triangle is going on!"

He pointed the spade at Justin. "Queen Revari is like a daughter to me. She's been through hell and back. She was right not to side with you when you foolishly teamed up with the one MaleForm who could've destroyed her and Platirius. If you have a psychic ability, you should've been able to feel a familial connection to Prince Dimaro before you unleashed him."

"But I saw something!" Justin shot back. "I saw him climb out of a grave."

"And that didn't give you a clue you shouldn't have entertained him? If you want my help, learn to treat the queen with respect. Until you apologize to her, we have nothing to talk about!"

He lifted an oversized crate on his shoulder and stormed off.

"Great," said Justin. "Now how am I going to put the pieces of the puzzle together?"

"**W**here the hell do you get off sticking your nose in my business?"

Justin looked up from entering prescriptions into the system at a furious Dr. Azini. The older physician didn't give him time to respond.

Pointing a finger at Justin's face, he said, "You arrived six months ago and no one knows who you are or where you came from. I tried to access your records, but the system denied my clearance. The system *I* designed for the practice *I* built from the ground up! And you, a stranger, have been granted the keys without so much as a heads-up from King Leighton!"

Dr. Azini snatched an apple off Justin's desk and waved it in the air. "These are MY patients in MY practice, yet you're walking around as if you're the head of this medical chamber! Oh, I checked into your supply list too. You get the best cuts of beef before they're offered to me and the freshest vegetables and fruit from the gardening chamber—you, a stranger!"

His eyes narrowed at Justin. "Who did you bribe to get in here?"

Justin watched Dr. Azini's tantrum unfold with a calmness that further enraged him.

"I didn't bribe anyone. I just showed up and started giving the patients the care they needed."

"That's right, you show up and all hell breaks loose. You convinced those little brats to lie on Vantra—the best mother they've ever had—now she's locked up on bogus charges. The justice council wouldn't let me post the fee to free her!"

"She doesn't deserve to walk around after what she did to the triplets. Neither do you."

Dr. Azini laughed. "Oh, that's rich. You thought you'd use those useless pups to bring me down too? I regret to inform you, Dr. Ascencio, but the justice council doesn't accept testimony from ChildForms under twelve summers against anyone outside of the family."

Hurling the apple at a wall, he said, "Furthermore, a commoner's word has never stood against a member of the elite and succeeded. You have a lot to learn about our planet if you think you'll come here and cause trouble! I won't be arrested today, tomorrow, or ten seconds after you die and go to hell. Too bad all of your hard work to steal my practice was for nothing."

"I wouldn't say it was all for nothing," said Justin. He nodded up into a corner.

Dr. Azini didn't take his eyes off of him. "Oh yes, I read the king's decree. Along with outside surveillance, we're forced to endure being monitored like babies who just learned to walk! So much for patient privacy."

"You don't care about your patients or their privacy," said Justin. "You're more concerned with covering your ass. I guess you won't be able to bend any WomenForms over exam tables anytime soon without getting caught, huh?"

Dr. Azini fumed. "You arrogant little prick! I want your desk cleared out before a half-hour's span, and I don't want to see you again. Am I understood?"

Justin leaned back in his chair and smiled. "I'm not going anywhere, Dr. Azini. I was given this position by the king. If you have an issue with me being here, I suggest you take it up with him."

"King Leighton doesn't decide what goes on at this medical chamber, I do."

Justin laughed in his face. "He's JanIus's king. He controls everything and everyone—including you."

He stood up, towering over Dr. Azini by several inches. "I'd love to see you inform the king of who he's in charge of."

Dr. Azini's jaw tightened. "You have no idea what you've just stepped into. I don't know who your connections are, nor do I care. I have friends in high places too. If you think you'll breeze in here and usurp me out of my position, I have news for you. If King Leighton won't get you out, I will."

Spinning on his heel, he snatched open the door. "You think you're some big shot because the king put you here, but not all of us support him! Any MaleForm—royal or commoner—who allows women to sit on justice councils has no business being in charge!"

He pointed at Justin. "It was a mistake to make an enemy out of me. You'd better watch your back!"

Turning to leave, he shouted, "Get out of my way!" at a NurseForm.

Justin hadn't realized he'd been clenching his teeth, something he did when he was furious. It looked as if Dr. Azini would get away with harming the triplets. He hadn't seen that coming. The more he thought about it, the angrier he became.

A dull ache began in his temples, mounting swiftly into a throbbing headache. He lowered his head—harsh breaths were coming strong and heavy. What was happening? He'd never had a headache before.

He hated uncleanliness. Willing himself to get up and retrieve a cloth to wipe up the mess, he paused when a sharp pain shot through his skull again. Rubbing his temples, he struggled to control his breathing.

He approached the wall, gripping a cleaning cloth firmly in his hand. Kneeling down to retrieve the apple made him a bit lightheaded. Swiftly tossing it into a disposal bin, he pivoted to wipe the stains from the wall when a peculiar, platinum light flashed in front of him.

What the hell?

He wiped his eyes, believing he was imagining things, but the light grew larger until it materialized in the form of a BrainStaff. Curiously, he stared at it, fixated, as if he were in a trance. The BrainStaff's power glowed brilliantly against the cream and mulberry-colored tapestry.

"*Kill him...*" whispered a voice. "*Kill him now...*"

Staring into the light, Justin saw the face of a young king. His wavy black hair fell a bit past his shoulders. A high crown of platinum and diamonds sat on his head, sharply contrasting with silk black robes. His sparkling onyx eyes bore into him with an evilness that made Justin nauseous.

"Who are you?" asked Justin.

"Who I am isn't relevant," said the king. "What I can do for you is more imperative."

This isn't happening, thought Justin. *That's what I get for skipping lunch.*

"Either you tell me who you are or you can haunt someone else. I have work to do."

"Oh yes. We have much to accomplish, Prince Justin. I am King Anemi, your great-grandfather. You're the last male descendant of my line."

Justin couldn't believe what he was seeing.

"You have immense power channeling inside of you. I can help you use it to get everything you desire."

Justin braced his hands on the wall, fascinated by the mysterious young king.

"Join me," he whispered. "Join me and take your rightful place as Platirius's king. Kill the doctor and King Leighton and take control of his planet. Absorb it into Platirius after you behead Queen Vivant. Platirius wasn't built for a wretched WomanForm to control it. You must end her. It is your birthright and your duty to uphold the throne."

The pounding in his head grew worse. Despite his best efforts, he couldn't escape from the dark, murky energy.

"No," he said, shaking his head violently. "I don't want to kill anyone! Get out of here and leave me alone!"

"Let me help you," said King Anemi. "Queen Vivant deserves to die for what she did to your family! Platirius is rightfully yours! Kill her and make Lyric your queen." The king smiled slyly. "That is what you want, isn't it? To have Lyric in your bed? You're the only one who can make Queen Vivant pay for what she did to your father."

Sweat poured down Justin's face. He had to get out of there!

"My sorcery was unsurpassed in my day. I can show you how to use your powers and claim your destiny. Accept my offer and you'll have everything you've ever wanted." King Anemi reached for Justin. "Take my hand," he whispered.

"No!" Justin shouted. Clutching his head in his palms, he desperately tried to reach the door. The furious flames inside his head roared. Holding it in his hands, he yelled, "My God! Someone help me, please!" he begged. "I need help in here!"

A NurseForm came rushing to the door. "Dr. Ascencio, what's wrong?"

He heard screaming just before he collapsed in front of her. Then everything went black.

J ustin was still unconscious by the time Gallium reached him. He watched the medical team lay him on a cool, chrome table.

Since he was part Coldarian, Gallium could hear his thoughts. *Please? Please help me! We have to stop him!*

He reached out, gripping his shoulder. "It's all right. It's Gallium. You're safe now."

Gallium! He's trying to use me. I won't let him!

Gallium leaned closer to him. "Who?" he whispered. "Who's trying to use you?"

But Justin's mind fell silent.

Dr. Corning entered and nodded at Gallium. "Are you assuming responsibility as his guardian? We don't know where he came from or whom to contact to obtain authorization for treatment."

"Yes, I will. I've known him for a long time."

Dr. Corning eyed him curiously. "Where does he come from?"

Gallium's eyes narrowed. "I can't tell you that, but I assure you, he's of high status. If I were you, I would treat him and fast."

The doctor nodded. "Alright, I'll take your word for it. We're running tests to determine what happened."

He rubbed his bald head. "To be honest, there's no reason for him to be unconscious. We scanned the surveillance in his office. After arguing with Dr. Azini, Dr. Ascencio sat at his desk for a moment. It looks as if he stood to leave just before he collapsed. He's young and strong. It doesn't make any sense."

A sinking feeling rose in Gallium's stomach. He had his suspicions, but prayed he was wrong. If the prince's silent enemies were who he thought they were, then no doctor could help him. He didn't know if anyone would be able to stop them.

*J*ustin awakened to see King Carlomon sitting across from him at a table. *I'm back in the dining chamber!* He felt an ominous presence he couldn't see. King Carlomon looked at him sadly.

"What are you trying to tell me, Great-Grandfather?"

The scene changed. Now he was standing in a small room. He whirled to see King Carlomon sitting in a chair, staring out a window. Blood from a wound in the king's arm pooled around Justin's feet.

Suicide? thought Justin.

The king's sad eyes sought his. "No," he whispered. "He killed us."

"Who? Who hurt you, King Carlomon? What really happened to Coldarius?"

The king's fingers found a small blue topaz on a chain around his neck. "It's gone. Find it. It's the only way to make things right."

Justin leaned forward to survey the exquisite stone. Looking up at King Carlomon, he said, "Make what right? What is this stone? Where is it now?"

The light slowly drained out of the king's eyes. "Enter the king," he whispered.

Justin looked up to see a dark figure standing in the doorway. It was the same presence he felt in the dining chamber.

"Who are you? Why did you murder King Carlomon?"

The figure slowly emerged from the shadows. A long blade glinted in the light. Two lions with tiny onyx eyes were carved on the handle above an elaborately engraved DA. The blade flashed through the air, tearing through the skin on his arm.

Noooooooooooooo!

Now he was on a craft hurling toward a breathtaking stretch of water. He smelled fumes from the damaged engine. Someone was standing at the motherboard, desperately trying to regain control of the craft. He turned to Justin. Beautiful violet-gray eyes he'd recognize anywhere stared back at him.

"Please save my Lyric."

"General Iham?"

He gritted his teeth at the monitors that blared loudly above his head. Sharp pain ripping through his skull made him wince. Feeling a warm hand cover his, he sighed when it extinguished the chill in his fingers. He turned his head away from the glaring lights, becoming lost in mesmerizing violet-gray pools again.

"Prince Justin?"

"Lyric," he murmured. "I have to save you. I promised your father."

Slipping back into the sea of unconsciousness, he gratefully allowed the waves to shield him from danger.

General Lyric bathed a cool cloth against his face. After hearing about the accident, she'd volunteered to be dispatched to JanIus. She tried to convince herself it was out of duty to her queen, but truth prevailed. She'd missed him.

Setting aside the cloth, she rose reluctantly from his side. She was due to report to her station in an hour. Before she could stop herself, she pressed her lips to his cool forehead.

"Stay the course, Prince Justin. Keep going. For me."

As she turned to leave, she looked back at his silent form.

How do you know my father's name?

A NurseForm watched her pass through the entrance of the medical chamber before placing a call.

"Yes?"

"She was here. She just left."

"Did he speak to her?"

"He said a name I didn't recognize—General Iham."

There was a long silence. "Your payment will be sent to you within an hour."

After the call disconnected, the NurseForm stood over Justin, watching him sleep.

Fawn's Past

Fawn could hardly contain her excitement. Today was the first day of class at Queen Vivant's elaborate instruction chamber.

71

When Colonel Angela, a high-ranking Revaltian, knocked on her door, she thought she'd faint. Her parents were so surprised that their mouths had literally dropped. Her father had been too intimidated by the stern, petite soldier to utter a sound.

"Queen Revari has selected your daughter for admission to her ParaNurture doctoral program. It would be wise to keep your mouth shut. If you don't, you'll be transferred to Revani to address your concerns in front of our queen. What's your pleasure?"

"Of c-course she can go," stammered her father.

Her mother sat quietly at the table, nervously wringing her hands.

Captain Angela's dark gaze cut into him. "A wise choice," she said.

"Fawn Azini, I've come to bring you to Platirius. You don't need to take any belongings. Everything you need will be provided for you. Let us go."

Without saying goodbye to her parents, Fawn got up and followed her.

Now she was sitting in a chamber filled with eager young WomenForms. She could barely contain her excitement. A pretty WomanForm with dark, wavy hair and skin the color of rich hazelnuts stood at the front of the classroom in front of a large TranScreen. Her brilliant white uniform, adorned with platinum medals, was neat and stylish. Fawn noted that she had a very pleasant smile.

"Welcome to the Platirius Institute for WomenForms. I'm your instructor, Captain TamRi."

Widening her stance, Captain TamRi folded her arms behind her back. "Congratulations. You have been selected for a very prestigious program. The Queen Dellah Amorous Scholarship isn't awarded to just any Being. You must have impeccable grades and a letter of recommendation with your application."

Fawn closed her eyes, silently thanking The One for Queen Vivant's kindness.

"Beyond that, you must be in peak physical condition. It takes years of dedication to become a ParaNurture physician. For too many years, WomenForms were shut out of doctoral studies, and as a result, many WomenForms perished, including the mother of our founders—Queen Dellah."

Fawn's eyes drifted to a large painting of Queen Dellah hanging high on the wall above Captain TamRi. She thought the fashionably dressed queen was stunning.

"Once we began adding our contributions to research, we noticed the rates of death drastically diminished. Now, only one in seven hundred thousand WomenForms die giving birth each year. There's a reason for that. We only select the best. Over the course of four summers, your training will be split between classroom instruction and physical training."

Fawn bit her lip with excitement. She'd always wanted to learn how to fight. If she could defend herself against her father, maybe he'd leave her and her mother alone.

"Once your studies are complete, you will be trained not only as medical professionals, but as members of an army. You'll earn credit for every class you enroll in and pass successfully. At the end of the program, a celebration feast will be held for all graduates on Revani."

Fawn held her breath and looked around the chamber. Judging from the expressions on her classmates' faces, they were just as anxious and excited as she was.

"I'll warn you ahead of time, there will be no room for error. However, if you work hard to impress the queens, your future will be brighter than you could ever imagine."

Captain TamRi smiled at the students. "Now, are you ready to save lives?"

A few murmurs echoed in the chamber. She cocked a hand to her ear. "I said, are you ready to save lives?"

A loud chorus of yesses filled the air.

Captain TamRi nodded. "That's better. Hold up your palms and let's begin."

She turned on a large TranScreen.

"You'll take your notes from everything on the screen in front of you. Be sure to be as detailed as possible and save them on the hard drives in your palms. You won't receive any refresher courses. If you're going to be competent physicians, having an efficient memory is your best asset."

"Ethics," read Captain TamRi. "Does anyone know why they're important?"

No one in the class volunteered to answer. Captain TamRi began walking up and down between the rows of seats.

"No one knows? Are you not at the top of your class ranks? Why is it important for a physician to have a sound comprehension of ethics?"

Fawn raised her hand. "If you don't have a sense of right or wrong, you could easily harm your patient."

"Excellent, Fawn. But I have fourteen hundred and twenty-five students in my course. Surely Fawn isn't the only one with something to contribute?"

"Show-off. Is she going to answer every question?" muttered Domi Cottes under her breath.

Captain TamRi crossed the classroom and stood in front of her. "If I were you, Domi Cottes, I would worry less about what Fawn says and more about what you're not saying. Those who don't pull their weight in class will be immediately dismissed from the program."

She leaned in to peer into Domi's face. "And once you're gone, an unsatisfactory report will be reviewed and signed by both queens and sent to your planet's Hall of Records. You won't be able to enroll in another program, nor will anyone hire you for work. Ever."

Captain TamRi's soft, confident tone filled the instruction chamber, so every student heard her. She waited, looking into Domi's face.

"Vivacians have no use for those who cannot get along with others. You will be assigned to an army of women whom you'll have to depend on. Now, do you have something useful to add, or should I have you shipped out of here right now?"

Domi cleared her throat. "Yes, Captain TamRi. I apologize for being unkind. If you don't respect the principles of doing what is right, then you'll become a liability to your community, not an asset."

"That's right, Domi!" said Captain TamRi, rapping her knuckles on the cool, chrome table.

"We're building a strong foundation for communities to thrive. We cannot afford to send liabilities into the medical field. Beings who break the rules and follow their own devices don't save lives, they ruin them."

She continued walking up the rows, surveying the students. "Make a special notation of this: Beings without a strong sense of ethics endanger the lives of their patients, causing irreparable harm to the medical community as a whole."

Fawn dutifully scanned notes on her palm until a flashing blue light chimed on the platinum wall. It was time to be dismissed for the luncheon break.

"Leave your belongings here and follow me to the dining chamber. We'll return in an hour."

Chapter 5

Platirius's dining chamber was overflowing with hungry students. Fawn watched Beings hurrying back and forth through its doors. She inhaled the tantalizing aromas and clutched her stomach when it gurgled. Self conscious and on high alert, she'd hoped no one had seen her, but Hadna Krunzel giggled.

"Hungry, huh? Me too! I've been dreaming about eating in Platirius's dining chamber for years." Bouncing up and down on her feet, she said, "Now I have the chance! I'm from Cassnah. Where are you from?"

Fawn had always been shy. Noting Hadna's long, dark hair and eyes, and her smooth olive skin, she let her eyes roam over her fashionable clothes. She suspected Hadna had grown up with privilege too.

"I'm from JanIus," she said.

"Oh, that's far from us," said Hadna. "I heard you have a good king. Ours is terrible. Had Queen Revari not sponsored the program, he would've issued a royal decree to prevent me from signing up. He hates smart WomenForms."

Hadna sighed. "I doubt if I'll be able to return as a physician. All of ours are MaleForms."

Fawn hadn't thought about where she'd be assigned. Her father's practice was thriving, but she doubted he'd allow her to assist him. Although many galactic kings didn't like the idea of educating WomenForms, they were reluctant to challenge Queen Vivant and Queen Revari. They didn't want their economies to suffer.

Since Prince Dimiro's attempt to conquer Platirius, neither queen allowed the other to fight royal MaleForms alone. When the Revaltians teamed up with the Vivacians, it remained the main topic of discussion around the galaxy for months.

"It's a good thing I don't have to decide where I want to go," said Hadna. "Lucky for us, there's lots of places that need skilled medical staff."

"I'm glad," said Fawn. "Even if I have to relocate, I'm sure I'll be sent to a good location."

"With even better financial perks," Hadna added. "I don't want to be paid less than MaleForms, so I'm grateful to have been chosen for this program. I hear the queens negotiated the employment funds to be equal to or more than what MaleForms get. If any ruler refused, they wouldn't receive financial assistance from their realms."

"That's good to hear," said Fawn. "I'm glad things are changing for the better."

"They are, but I suspect we'll have opposition, even if it's covert. MaleForms are sneaky, you know?"

Hadna clapped her hands together once, rubbing them with anticipation. "Let's eat, Fawn! I'm hungry!"

They selected their trays and eating utensils when Fawn spotted Domi. Quickly, she turned her head and focused on the numerous pans of food inside the tall, chrome tables.

"I wouldn't worry about her," said Hadna. "Captain TamRi put the fear of The One into her. No one is crazy enough to get kicked out of the program."

Fawn sighed. She hoped Hadna was right. Without a recommendation for education or vocation, Beings often had no choice but to leave for Earth. Going to Earth without proper support often meant inevitable death.

The Humans' food was detestable and the stench of them was worse. Fawn didn't wish that fate on anyone—not even a Being as mean-spirited as Domi seemed to be.

"Well, young WomenForms," said Dora Reese. "Make sure you eat your fill today. We worked hard to prepare all of this just for you."

She pointed to rows of tables heavily laden with desserts. "I make the best cakes on Platirius. No one does them better, and if they say they do, they're lying!"

Her jovial laugh made Fawn and Hadna smile. Dora's reddish-brown skin was smooth and line-free, with only a few strands of gray peeking out from sandy-brown hair. Her kind, oval-shaped eyes were the color of bright copper. A dash of freckles on her nose and cheeks made her look quite young.

Suddenly, a hush fell over the dining chamber. Dora stopped smiling when she saw who entered. Queen Revari strolled in with General Legend and Colonel Sheila flanking her sides. Dressed in red attire and high heels, the Revaltians were an impressive sight. To Fawn, they seemed to glide across the floor.

Queen Revari abruptly stopped in front of Dora, staring her down. "I heard you had a lot to say about me when I was on Earth, old WomanForm," she said softly.

Quickly, Dora bowed to her. "Me? Oh! I meant no harm. Please forgive me. I tend to talk out of turn sometimes."

"Lift your head when you speak to me, Dora Reese," commanded Queen Revari.

Trembling, she did as she was told. Queen Revari's icy, silver eyes sliced through her before attempting to go around her.

"Forgive me, Queen Dellah. I made your favorite peach pie. It's sitting right over there."

Queen Revari stilled. Peering into Dora's face, she surveyed her curiously for a few seconds. "What did you just call me?"

Dora's smile was too wide and she had a faraway look in her eyes. "Queen Dellah. Your wedding to King Dubian is still the grandest anyone's ever seen. You've been good to us, My Queen. I don't want to do anything to upset you."

Fawn felt a chill. Something was wrong. She'd never met Dora Reese or any of the other powerful WomenForms, but she felt Dora wasn't the type to mistake one Being for another.

The scowl on Queen Revari's face softened into concern as Queen Vivant approached the group. She, too, had overheard

JANIUS PAWNS BOOK I

Dora's words. She nodded to Fawn and Hadna, "Please report to lunch and return to class on time."

Fawn and Hadna hurried to pile food onto their trays and find good seats. Everyone except the queens, General Legend, and Colonel Sheila focused on eating and talking quietly with each other.

"Dora?" asked Queen Vivant. "Do you think this is Queen Dellah?"

Dora smiled. "Of course! I'd know her anywhere. She's the finest queen Platirius has ever had. Much better than that nasty Queen Zherta!"

She turned to Queen Vivant. "You won't tell her I said so, will you?"

Queen Vivant shook her head. "No, I won't, Dora, but who am I?"

Absently surveying the queen, she said, "Well...I don't know. You look familiar, but I can't recall when we've met."

"Dora," said Queen Revari. "Why don't you cut a big slice of pie for me, and I'll take it with me into my meeting?"

Dora's face beamed. "Just a slice, Your Majesty? I made a whole pie just for you. You and the new little one can have it all. You're not showing yet, but give it some time. You'll be as big as you were when Princess Vivant was born. There's no shame in having a bit of meat on your bones, if you don't mind me speaking my mind, Your Highness."

Queen Vivant tried to interject, but Queen Revari raised her hand to stop her from interrupting.

Flashing a radiant smile at Dora, she said, "Not at all. It would be a sad day if you lost your wit. It's what I respect most about you. Very well, bring the whole pie. Everyone knows you're the best baker on my staff."

Dora grinned at Queen Revari. "I'll get it right now, Your Highness!" she said, hurrying toward the desserts.

Queen Revari's smile slowly faded as she met Queen Vivant's eyes. "Why haven't you handled this, Vivant?"

Queen Vivant's eyebrow arched. "As you can see, I've just learned about it."

But Queen Revari wasn't letting her off the hook. "She's one of the oldest Platirians we have left—one of the few who still remembers Mother. How could you allow her brain to deteriorate? If you focused more on your subjects than trying to get into King Asa's pants, maybe you could've addressed it sooner."

Queen Vivant bristled. "Revari, my personal life is none of your business. Maybe if you allowed yourself to have a male companion, you'd relax a bit."

Queen Revari smirked. "Why? So you can kill him and ship him into the sun too?"

"You're a lot better at killing MaleForms than I am!" quipped Queen Vivant.

Queen Revari's red gaze penetrated her. "Tsk. Oh, big sister. You have no idea just how good I am at that!"

She raised a single finger and raked her nail in the air, stopping short of touching Queen Vivant's face.

JANIUS PAWNS BOOK I

General Legend and Colonel Sheila smirked. Although Queen Vivant didn't, they knew exactly whom Queen Revari was referring to.

Queen Vivant sighed deeply. "We're supposed to meet to discuss the curriculum for the doctoral program. I don't have the energy to fight with you today, Revari. When are you going to let it go?"

"Ten thousand years after I die and go to hell—that's when I'll let it go. Not a second sooner."

Queen Vivant rolled her eyes toward the ceiling.

"Where are my mother's photos?" asked Queen Revari.

"*Our* mother's photos are in my bed chamber. I'd like to go over them with you before the day ends."

"I don't need you looking over my shoulder when I see them," said Queen Revari dryly. "I'm not a ChildForm anymore."

Queen Vivant sighed. "Will you at least try to be reasonable today? We need to set a good example for the students."

Queen Revari wrinkled her nose. "I see no reason to put on airs. They'll learn exactly who I am when they come to Revani for training."

She looked at Dora, who had returned with the warm pie. Dora's face was etched with worry when she handed the pie to Queen Revari.

"Young WomanForm, you shouldn't speak to Queen Dellah that way," she said to Queen Vivant. "She's a kind soul, but she'll cut you down for disrespecting her. And don't get me started on

King Dubian. He's crazy about her. He'll have you stripped and beaten in front of everyone."

The WomenForms were stunned by what they heard. They were genuinely saddened that Dora's mind had reverted back in time—especially Queen Revari. Dora didn't know she'd earned her respect by showing loyalty to her mother and grandfather, King Carlomon.

"You have the power of Healing to help her. Use it," Queen Revari whispered to Queen Vivant. "Her body is still strong. There's no reason she should spend her life with her mind wandering in the dark like the Humans."

Balancing the pie perfectly on her palm, she said, "We've never had brain diseases. I see no reason to start now."

She glanced at Dora again. "I'd rather have her call me a spawn of the devil than not remember who I am. Let us go."

Without another word, she, General Legend, and Colonel Sheila left Queen Vivant standing with Dora.

"Come, Dora," said Queen Vivant. "We have a bit of time before my meeting starts. Let's get you feeling better, yes?"

D ora followed Queen Vivant into her wellness chamber.
"Sit down in front of me," said Queen Vivant.

Gingerly, she placed her fingers on Dora's temples. Flashes of memories of when Queen Vivant was a baby and of her childhood flowed from Dora's mind to hers. Dora's memories flew by at record speed until she saw Dora standing with a crowd of mourners outside the palace, wailing over Queen Dellah's death.

Next, she saw Dora rejoicing over King Dubian's death. She scanned Dora's memories of her wedding and the birth of her ChildForms, then to mourning the princesses at their DeathCeremony.

She combed through Dora's mind, pausing to stop at one that caught her attention. Queen Revari, dressed in old Platirian armor, entered General Kron's personal craft. She couldn't make sense of it, so she filed it away for later.

She restored all of her memories after extracting a black tumor that was positioned on her brain. The repulsive mass pulsated rapidly in the palm of her hand.

"Alzheimer's disease," she said, bewildered by the discovery. "This is a Human malady. How could it have affected Dora?"

She turned to push a button on her desk.

"Sonee, come to my wellness chamber and bring a specimen capsule. I have a mystery I want you to solve with the group of students I'm assigning to you."

"Of course, Your Highness. I'll be right there."

Dora was still in a deep sleep by the time Sonee appeared to collect the sample. She awakened shortly after she left.

"Goodness fox! What on Platirius am I doing in here?"

Queen Vivant smiled at her. "I brought you here to talk about the supper menu, Dora. But you were so tired, you fell asleep."

Dora frowned sadly. "I'm awfully sorry, Queen Vivant. I hope you don't think I'm rude."

"It's no problem at all. In fact, you did such an amazing job putting out a spread for the students, I'm ordering you to take the rest of the day off. Go home and get some rest. I won't hear any objections. Have I been heard?"

"Yes, My Queen. I think I'd like that very much."

She got up to leave. "Oh, and Queen Vivant?"

"Yes, Dora?"

"I heard Queen Revari was coming to the meeting. You'll make sure she won't see me, right? I don't want her to be mad at me about what I said when she was on Earth. I didn't mean any of it." Dora shuffled her feet. "I love her just as much as I love you. I've just never known how to talk to her. She's... She has quite a temper, so I never know what to say to her."

Queen Vivant smiled at her. "Don't worry, Dora. I have a feeling the two of you won't cross paths today."

Dora bowed to her. "Thank you, Queen Vivant—a long life to you and Queen Revari. And if you don't mind me saying it, your mother and grandfather would be so proud of both of you if they were still with us. King Carlomon, I mean. Not King Anemi."

Unconsciously, she shrank back from the large painting of him above Queen Vivant's desk. "Forgive me for saying this, but I don't think anyone misses him."

Queen Vivant blinked back tears. Unlike Queen Revari, her memories of their Coldarian family were crystal clear.

"I understand what you mean. Not a day goes by that I don't miss them. And Aunt Opal too."

Dora nodded. "I didn't always agree with her, but she did right by you and your sister."

Queen Vivant glanced at the painting of Queen Opal. "Yes, she did. I often wonder how our lives would've turned out had she lived."

The crystal timekeeper chimed softly. "Well, I have to get to my meeting, and you have a date with some rest! Please enjoy the rest of your day."

"You too, Your Highness."

Dora smiled and turned her back on King Anemi's searing gaze, staring down at her in hatred.

The tension had been building since Queen Vivant sat down at the head of the table. She thought holding the meeting in the library would provide a more comfortable atmosphere than the stoic meeting chamber their father had built, but she was wrong.

General Lyric, Captain TamRi, and Major Sonee flanked her right and left sides, while General Legend and Colonel Sheila sat at the far end of the table with Queen Revari.

"Thank you for coming. I believe the ParaNurture doctoral program will prove to be very beneficial not only for our students, but to the advancement of WomenForms as a whole."

Queen Revari, nibbling on a slice of pie, said nothing. That didn't surprise Queen Vivant. Her sister had never been much of a talker, so that didn't worry her. Yet, her mind continuously raced without pausing for rest. That frightened her. A lot.

"Has Dora Reese been healed?" asked General Legend.

Queen Vivant nodded curtly. "Yes, I extracted a medium-sized mass from her brain. It's a Human disease. Alzheimer's."

"How on Platirius was she affected by that?" asked General Lyric.

"I have no idea, but I suspect it came from the last Human sentenced to the Flames of Justice—Kyle Kaufman," said Queen Vivant. "He didn't last twenty-four hours after I ordered his release. His brain shut down in seconds."

Queen Revari pushed her plate away. "Then it's a no-brainer, no pun intended." Her steely gaze left no room for opposition. "You should kill all of the Humans imprisoned on Platirius. We can't allow their diseases to poison the rest of us."

"I have a more humane approach than that," said Queen Vivant.

"I can't wait to hear it," said Queen Revari dryly.

"We'll use Kaufman's body as a cadaver for the research students. They'll work with Major Sonee to discover the origin of the disease—whether he had it when he arrived from Earth or if it developed while imprisoned. They'll also be tasked with the responsibility of finding out how it affected one of our own. The rest of the Humans will be shipped back to Earth."

"So you're just going to allow the Humans to fly across our solar system, poisoning our atmosphere instead of extinguishing them," said Queen Revari.

It wasn't a question. Her statement dripped with disapproval of Queen Vivant's idea.

"I see no reason to take their lives, Queen Revari," said Queen Vivant.

"Even if it means protecting our own Beings from them? What do you think will happen once they return to Earth? They'll tell someone, and their idiotic leaders will try to discover where we are."

Wiping her hands on an embroidered napkin, she said, "There's already one idiot in the United States who's obsessed with Space. I'd kill him, but I haven't had the time. Dora Reese may not have been the only one affected. We're not responsible for caring for Humans over our race!"

"I'm the Protector of Earth as well as Platirius, sister!"

Crimson fire blazed in Queen Revari's eyes. "And you wear it like a badge of honor, don't you? You're so proud of your little title that it's gone to your head, inflating your already suffocating ego. I didn't think you could fall more deeply in love with yourself than you already are."

"Despite what you think of me, this program was founded in our mother's honor. We're here to educate young female students so that what happened to her won't happen again.

I am just as committed as you to preserving and protecting WomenForms."

"Then kill the Humans and be done with it," snapped Queen Revari.

"I won't, and you know I won't, so stop telling me what to do. I only kill when I'm forced to. I don't enjoy it as much as you."

Queen Revari shook her head and sucked her teeth. "Then let's get on with this. I'm only able to take you in small doses."

"Fine," said Queen Vivant. "As you know, we have fourteen hundred and twenty-five females who'll receive a scholarship to enter our program. They are the best and the brightest from planets around the galaxy. We need to finalize the curriculum one last time."

"The program's length has been broken down into four summers—two on Platirius and two on Revani," said Colonel Sheila. "Since they'll be taught using the principles discovered in Queen Dellah's journals, I think it would be good to alternate the time. I'm on board with having the students spend the first two summers on Platirius before training with me for the final two on Revani."

General Legend raised her hand. "I agree with Colonel Sheila. They need to understand that although the Revaltians have a different fighting style than the Vivacians, Queen Dellah's philosophies are the same and they should be abided by no matter what planet they're on."

Queen Vivant tossed a frosty glance at General Legend, but General Lyric said, "I agree. Queen Dellah's journals are extremely detailed. Queen Dellah trained General Legend, but we both received training under General Kron. It's best if the students learn both methods."

Queen Vivant scanned a document on her palm. Pushing her glasses up on her nose, she said, "I see here you want Gallium teaching the students?" she asked Queen Revari. "Why? He's a MaleForm."

"He's also the best at making chemical weapons," said Queen Revari. "No one in the galaxy, including Platirius, knows how to emulate him. He's been doing it since Mother and Grandfather hired him to. Passing on his knowledge to the students will help them, not hurt them. My Revaltians have benefited from his tutelage many times over."

"Oh? How so?" asked Queen Vivant.

Queen Revari smiled at her evilly, yet kept quiet.

"You mean when you tried to take over Earth and failed. We are training them to save lives, not commit murder," said Queen Vivant.

"The females will be soldiers and physicians. Learning how to defend yourself is vital to sustaining life. Or would you rather they end up like Dr. Krause?"

Queen Vivant shook her head. "That's in the past. Father isn't here to persecute WomenForms anymore."

"Will you take your head out of your behind for a moment?" asked Queen Revari. "There are thousands of kings just like King Dubian who absolutely despise WomenForms. You and I are the only two queens powerful enough to run planets. Why do you think that is? Because everywhere, misogynistic MaleForms have their feet on the necks of WomenForms. They can't heal their way out of tyranny!"

She expanded her arms wide. "They have to learn how to defend themselves if they're going to be successful. Just because you've decided to allow MaleForms on Platirius again, it doesn't mean the rest of us share your sentiments toward them. What good is it to train WomenForms to save their peers if they're limited in defending themselves?"

Queen Revari pushed back her chair and crossed her legs. "Even with everything that's happened since Mother died, you still believe MaleForms are decent. I don't."

"You don't?" asked Queen Vivant. "Then why do you have one on your team?"

"Gallium is the exception to the rule. He was loyal to Mother and he's been loyal to me. He would've remained loyal to you, too, had you not sided with King Dubian and your arrogant husband!"

Queen Vivant removed her glasses and pointed them at Queen Revari. "They were my family—not Gallium."

"Yes," hissed Queen Revari. "A family that placed you above everyone and everything. There was no way you'd turn your back on that and fight back against the tyranny your father imposed on the rest of us."

Queen Vivant waved her hand dismissively. "Our father's way of running Platirius died with him. How long will you go on living in the past, Revari?"

"If we don't learn from our history, we'll be doomed to repeat it. That's something you've never been able to understand. Do you really think the old kings are gone from Platirius's grounds? They're not! They'll never leave as long as Platirius stands. Your misguided dreams of peace are nothing more than silly delusions. I don't care what you think of Gallium. He's staying on this committee."

An image of Prince Justin flashed in General Lyric's mind. She wanted to ask how he was faring, but didn't think it would be wise to do so in front of Queen Revari.

She cleared her throat. "If the students learn how to create chemical weapons, we can be sure they'll know how to protect themselves. It'll be one less thing to worry about, right, Queen Vivant?"

Queen Vivant nodded. Since Gallium would train the students on Revani, there'd be no chance of her getting close to Callidut again. She couldn't think of a reason to exclude him from the program.

"All right," said Queen Vivant. "Captain TamRi and Colonel Sheila, here are the schedules for the students. Major Sonee, I would like you to investigate the origin of the disease and explore potential cures. The generals will provide combat training for the students. I'm looking forward to working together as a unified team for the duration of the program."

She looked pointedly at Queen Revari. "It would be beneficial not to argue in front of the students. I want to set a good example of showing them proper communication skills and effective teamwork firsthand. I'll need your assistance."

Queen Revari had just polished off her second slice of peach pie. Licking the spoon, she set it down on the saucer with a soft clink. "Of course. The program is in Mother's honor. I can play nice until it's over. But if I do, I want something in return."

Queen Vivant, General Lyric, and Captain TamRi braced themselves. "And what would that be?" Queen Vivant asked.

"Now that Dora Reese is better, I'd like for her to bake a peach pie for me once a week. If I have to see you more often than I'd like, I'll need my sweet tooth satisfied."

Queen Vivant grinned at her. "I thought you'd ask for expensive jewelry or something more extravagant."

Queen Revari flexed her wrist, showing off an exquisite bracelet. "I have plenty of that. The bakers on Revani are skilled, but there's only one Dora Reese."

Queen Vivant sighed with relief. "You've got it. Peach pie it is. Does anyone else have anything else to add? No? Then we'll meet once a month to discuss any issues or concerns and the students' progress. Meeting adjourned."

Hadna and Fawn stretched out their legs over leisurely bites of the delicious luncheon. Hadna's tray was loaded with turkey meatloaf, fluffy mashed potatoes riddled with rich butter, and fresh, crisp green beans with bits of ham.

Fawn had chosen chicken and noodle soup in a creamy broth, along with a baked potato topped with broccoli, bacon, cheddar cheese, and sour cream. They both decided on thick slices of luscious lemon cake with cream cheese icing that practically melted in their mouths, accompanied by velvety smooth vanilla ice cream for dessert. Domi nervously approached them with her tray.

"If it's not a bother, may I sit with you?" she asked.

"Sure," said Fawn, moving over to make room for her.

Hesitantly, she sat down. Giving Fawn and Hadna a wary look, she said, "Listen, Fawn, I'm really sorry about what I said. I had to hear a ton of nonsense from my sister about not making the cut, so I was a bit on edge. I didn't mean to take my anger out on you."

Fawn read the sincerity in her eyes and smiled. "It's okay, Domi. We all have our days—even me."

"But you always seem so calm," said Domi.

"It may look that way on the outside," said Fawn. "But I have a lot of pent-up anger inside me too. I'm hoping I'll learn how to get rid of it before the last day of the program. I don't want to say or do anything that will jeopardize me becoming a physician."

Domi nodded. "I hear you. Me either." She lifted a cool mug of lemonade. "To friends?"

Fawn and Hadna smiled at each other and lifted their mugs. "To friends!"

Chapter 6

Captain TamRi stood at head of the classroom with a petite WomanForm Fawn didn't recognize. Her dark brown hair was almost black. The silver-rimmed glasses that sat over her light gold eyes had small, flashing lights on either side.

"I hope you all had a good lunch and are ready to learn," said Captain TamRi.

She pointed to a large, octagon-shaped building next to the instruction chamber. "The new wing of the instruction chamber was specifically designed for our ParaNuture students. It is where you'll learn, eat, and sleep. The week's end days are yours to do as you please."

Fawn was fascinated by the numbers shooting across the WomanForm's glasses.

"Queen Vivant is strict on clean environments, so please remember not to make unnecessary messes. Our cleaning staff rotates on twelve-hour shifts."

Captain TamRi smiled and nodded at the dark-haired WomanForm.

"Hello, students, I'm Major Sonee. Four hundred and twenty-five students will become research staff. The queens have designed a special project for the research students to work on. Due to its urgency, the Instruction Council that Captain TamRi and I sit on has decided that the research students will be taught separately from the ParaNurture students."

Fawn wondered which students had been chosen as research assistants. She hoped it wasn't any of the friends she'd made. Being a loner for all of her life, she'd grown attached to some of her peers.

"If there's a silver folder on your desk, please rise and follow me. My classroom is right across the hall from Captain TamRi's," said Major Sonee.

Fawn sighed with relief as the research students collected their belongings and followed Major Sonee into the classroom. They'd still eat and play games together.

"Alright. That's been taken care of. Let's begin," said Captain TamRi. She waved her hand and writing materialized in the air.

"Galactic Being Anatomy vs. Human Anatomy. Who can tell me why it's imperative to identify distinctions between our bodies and the Human body properly? Yes, Hadna?"

"We're not made like Humans."

Captain TamRi approached a large platinum desk and sat on top of it. "Explain."

"Human women have one womb while we have two. One of our wombs houses and nurtures an InfantForm until it reaches maturity, and the other stores the placenta and another sac—a *baniote*—which stores all of the nutrients needed by both the MotherForm and her InfantForm."

"What happens if the blood vessels inside the *baniote* rupture inside the second womb?" asked Captain TamRi.

"Unless it's removed in time, the MotherForm will die," said Hadna.

"What about the InfantForm? Will it die?"

"Only if it isn't taken out of the first womb before the blood in the second womb fills it. If an InfantForm is left inside the MotherForm for too long, it'll drown in blood."

"Correct," said Captain TamRi. "Very good, Hadna. Now, how many fetuses can our wombs hold versus a Human womb?"

The class went silent.

"The Humans believe there's no limit to the number of fetuses a Human woman's womb can hold. According to research, in 1971, a Human womb held up to fifteen fetuses. However, the possibility of Human women carrying this amount to full term is non-existent."

The captain waved her hand again. The students looked up at the words hovering in the air.

"In Earth's time of 1971, 15 fetuses, called quindecaplets, were removed from the womb of a 35-year-old mother four months after conception. Had they not been removed, both they and the mother would've perished. Humans are not equipped to handle what comes easily to our bodies."

The words moved in a carousel while the students furiously recorded notes onto their palms.

"The largest threat to a pregnant Human mother is an overabundance of mass. If the volume enlarges beyond a safe capacity, it compromises her ability to breathe. Other safety factors are hypertension and pre-eclampsia. Take note of the definitions for both terms. They'll be on your final examination."

After three hours had passed, a knock at the door interrupted her. A WomanForm with silver hair and a bright smile stuck her head inside the doorway.

"Busy shaping minds today, Captain TamRi? I brought the snacks and wanted to introduce myself to the young WomenForms. Moving forward, they'll be delivered through that chute."

She pointed to a highly polished chrome slot on the left side of the room.

Captain TamRi smiled at her. "Your timing is perfect. I think we could all use a good snack."

The visitor's warm smile made the students feel at ease. "Oh, good! Hello, students! I'm QiTan and I'm second-in-command of our dining chamber. We prepared something very special for you on your first day."

A floating robot pushing an enormous chrome cart followed her into the classroom. It approached Fawn and opened the cart to reveal a bevy of elaborately made parfaits with rich chocolate, banana, and strawberry puddings, crushed cookies, and generous amounts of whipped cream piled high in tall, crystal containers.

There were also squares of thick, fudgy brownies or decadent caramel blondies, and large containers of milk in various flavors. Fawn grabbed a chocolate parfait, a brownie, and a banana-flavored milk.

"Say thank you, Fawn," the robot cheerfully prompted.

Fawn's mouth dropped. Embarrassed, she looked around at everyone in the room.

"My apologies. I didn't know this model spoke."

QiTan smiled at her. "Oh yes, we have state-of-the-art friends who assist us in all of the chambers. This is Farah 2000."

"Thank you, Farah 2000," said Fawn. "But how did she know my name?"

"We entered all of your profiles into our system," said QiTan. "Every machine in the dining chamber knows who you are, your likes and dislikes, including food allergies. Our programming is very sophisticated and advanced compared to Human technology."

"You're welcome, Fawn," said Farah 2000 before going to each of the excited students to pass out their snacks.

Once everyone had taken all of the snacks, Farah 2000 closed the cart's door and floated toward QiTan.

"I hope you'll enjoy the food. Everyone involved in our program wants you all to succeed. Your bedtime snacks will be delivered via a chute located in your bed chambers. Just empty the carts and hit the button to return them to the dining chamber. If there's anything you need, please don't hesitate to contact us so we can properly address it."

"Thank you, QiTan. We're going to enjoy this," said Captain TamRi. "All right, students, you have twenty minutes to eat.

Farrah 2000 will be stationed outside and will return to collect your dishes and trash."

QiTan made a quick exit as the students dug into their food. After Farrah 2000 made her final rounds, they were ready to continue with the lesson.

"Another term you should know for the exam is hyperovulation. A Human mother in Uganda became pregnant fifteen times and birthed forty-four children between the Human years of 1993 to 2016. Humans consider this an anomaly, but we don't."

Captain TamRi stood from her chair and stretched. "Our wombs can hold up to thirty fetuses after conception and can be successfully birthed at a single time without complications."

Fawn raised an eyebrow. Even though her father was a doctor, she'd never heard of that.

"However, just because something can be done, that doesn't mean it should be. Can anyone give me an example of a long-term complication of allowing a WomanForm to birth thirty InfantForms at once?"

The class waited. No one wanted to look foolish if they gave the wrong answer.

Captain TamRi waited too. "All right. Here it is. The WomanForm who is permitted to birth that many InfantForms has the ability to populate her own world. If her ChildForms become too numerous, they could become their own army. They may turn distant toward other LifeForms and perhaps even hostile. The limited number we can birth is ten InfantForms at one time—no more."

Fawn couldn't imagine having that many siblings.

"Although we all live on different planets, we learn at a young age how to connect with each other and foster relationships based on mutual respect and effect communication. Does it always work? No. But this way of thinking has been successful since the beginning of our creation."

Captain TamRi carefully searched the faces of each student. "No one population should ever become so powerful they can wipe out other Beings in the blink of a star. The second issue is procreation. It is prohibited for family members to procreate with each other."

Fawn hadn't realized she was clenching her fist. Inbreeding disgusted her.

"On Earth, genetic deformities have occurred along with a lowered level of intellect for the Human species. This is why we're against it. We don't ever want to diminish our intellect to the level of Humans. To do so would be disgraceful to our races and communities."

Another student, Berea, raised her hand. "Has this ever happened before in Space?"

"Yes," said Captain TamRi. "A brother and sister procreated with each other, and the WomanForm became pregnant. Both were executed. Immediately."

Observing their shocked expressions, Captain TamRi said, "Now you may think that was harsh, but the galaxy has strict rules. We are above Humans with good reason. We intend to remain that way. Any threat to our way of life must be dealt with swiftly and efficiently."

The captain looked at the timekeeper on her wrist.

"And that's all for today," said Captain TamRi. "When you hear the chime, please report to the dining chamber for dinner, then proceed to the field behind this building. There are multiple TranScreens in the student bed chambers to watch programs. Our most popular channel is HumanFlix."

Hadna grinned excitedly at Fawn. She knew what that meant. They'd get to enjoy watching the Humans make fools of themselves.

"We also have tons of gaming machines and books to enjoy for a few hours of leisure before you have an evening snack and prepare for bathing and bed."

The students didn't know how to interpret Captain TamRi's teasing smile.

"But not on combat training days. After General Lyric finishes with you, you'll have just enough energy to shower and crawl into bed."

Fawn's curiosity was piqued about the physical training. *Will it really be that brutal?*

"Every morning, you'll report to the dining chamber for breakfast. Following the second chime of the day, I expect all of you to be standing before me and ready to begin your lessons. Tomorrow we'll be in the research chamber where you'll work on real cadavers—galactic and Human."

The students gasped and looked around at each other anxiously.

On cue, the chime rang sharply. "Class is dismissed," announced Captain TamRi.

Domi plopped down at the table with a plate loaded with thick slices of meatloaf, creamy, buttery mashed potatoes, and roasted broccoli. Fawn's selection of tender slices of turkey, cornbread dressing, candied carrots, and parsnips had her mouth watering.

Opting for a low-key dinner, Hadna chose a couple slices of pepperoni and sausage pizza with cottage fries. For dessert, they all opted for deep skillets of luscious ice cream bubbling over steaming, giant chocolate chip cookies.

"My brain feels fried," wailed Domi. "I've never had so many terms thrown at me in all of my lifespan!"

"Captain TamRi is excellent at what she does!" Hadna gushed. "I like her passion. Preparing us to take the ParaNurture final examinations on the first day of class is a genius idea! If we study hard and listen to her, we'll do well."

Domi frowned at her. "I'm glad one of us is optimistic," she said glumly.

"Oh, come on, Domi," said Fawn. "You got here just like the rest of us—because you had the top grades. You'll be fine." She smiled at her new friends. "We all will. We're going to be the best ParaNurture physicians in the galaxy!"

Hadna took a hefty bite of her pizza. "Are you going to work with your father in his practice, Fawn?"

Now it was Fawn's turn to frown. "I don't think so. I want to set up my own. I think it would be better if I could serve my patients my way without having to constantly look over my shoulder."

Her friends noted her sad expression, but didn't press her. They made plans for the end of the week, wolfed down their dinners, and reported to the training field.

The expansive training field had neatly clipped platinum grass as far as the eye could see. To the right were rows of old swords resting on a high bench. Lying next to the swords were weapons Fawn had never seen before.

A tall, beautiful WomanForm with short-cropped, sandy brown hair and violet-gray eyes stood in the center of the field. She was dressed in a snug, platinum battle suit. One of the strange weapons hung on her right hip, and a long, beautifully crafted sword protruded from her left.

The white and platinum athletic shoes she wore looked comfortable, but her serious expression made the students slow their pace right before they reached her. She carefully scanned each of their faces, taking note of every detail.

"I'm General Lyric, the leader of the Vivacian army."

Impressed by her confidence and carriage, the students exchanged glances. Fawn's eyes were drawn to the unidentified, highly polished weapon again.

"It's an Azgoate," muttered General Lyric. She removed it from her hip, enjoying the feel of its weight in her hand. "You're being trained to save the lives of pregnant WomenForms. But what happens when a MaleForm tries to end yours? It's my job to teach you how to arm and defend yourselves against an attack."

She uncovered something hidden under a platinum and cream cloth. The students gasped at what they saw. A large, crystal stone glowed brilliantly under the sunlight. Fawn was fascinated by the captivating rays of platinum, blue, crimson, and amethyst radiating from the stone.

"This," said General Lyric, nodding her head toward the stone, "is the Milan of Honor. On the night of the graduation ceremony, you'll all stand before it."

The stone's vibrant rays highlighted the violet hues in her eyes.

"Since King Dubian's death, being a warrior is something WomenForms have become accustomed to all over the galaxy. It's not enough to have a profession that finances your lifestyle."

She returned the Azgoate to her hip. "There are still many kingdoms that don't believe WomenForms should have the freedom to govern their own lives. At any time, the planet you'll be dispatched to after your training is over could be attacked."

Unsheathing her sword from the scabbard, she raised it high in the air. "This is the only thing that stands between living life on your own terms and becoming some MaleForm's unwilling wife, or worse, his prisoner."

Domi hiccupped and quickly covered her mouth, embarrassed by the interruption. General Lyric moved and stood directly in front of her, her sword still raised.

"Once you stand before the Milan of Honor, it will glow in different hues. Platinum means you'll become a Vivacian and train under me. If the light turns crimson, you'll become a member of the Revaltians—General Legend's army. JanIus's home color is violet. All JanIan soldiers report to King Leighton, who reports to a higher authority."

Fawn was puzzled by her statement.

Who's higher than a king?

The general caught Fawn in her line of sight. "Now, just because you were born on JanIus, that doesn't mean you'll end up living there. The Milan of Honor reads your heart to determine where you'll be an asset. Once you're stationed on a planet, you never leave. You will swear an oath to defend and protect the WomenForms you'll serve. Are there any questions?"

Domi raised her hand. "What about the MaleForms?"

General Lyric's sharp gaze assessed her. "What about them?"

"Well... On many of the planets—JanIus, Onzi, Platz—some of the citizens are MaleForms. Won't we have to protect them too?"

General Lyric cocked her head and slid the point of her sword to the side of Domi's neck. Fawn, Hadna, and the other students held their breath.

"And why would you think of protecting MaleForms over your Sisters?" growled General Lyric. "Do you think they'd risk their necks to protect us?"

Domi's eyes widened. "No! But—"

She looked around helplessly at her peers, desperate for assistance. All eyes stared straight ahead.

"I'm waiting to hear your answer, Student 304," pressed General Lyric.

"I don't know!" Domi cried. "I just thought..."

Her voice trailed off in despair.

General Lyric slowly lowered the sword. "Your way of thinking needs to change. And fast. Placing the needs of MaleForms over your SexForm will get them killed. Unlike JanIus, on Platirius, the MaleForms are peaceful. They live alongside us, but many of us WomenForms were content with the way things were before Pletz absorbed into Platirius."

Her cold, violet-gray eyes bore into Domi. "I won't say I despise MaleForms anymore, but I sure as hell don't trust many of them. If you're going to pass training with me, you'd best follow that line of thinking, or else you're no good to any WomanForms—on any planet. Is that understood, Student 304?"

"Yes," whispered Domi.

"Yes, General Lyric," she snapped crisply. "Speak up and always salute your commander when you're addressed!"

"Yes, General Lyric," Domi shouted, giving her a sharp salute.

"That's better," said General Lyric. "Any other questions?"

Another student, Raddie, raised her hand. "I thought Platz and Pletz were the same planet. Is that true?"

General Lyric shook her head. "No. As I said, Pletz was absorbed into Platirius. Platz is controlled by a king who's also a physician. Since none of you will be assigned there, you don't need to worry about it."

The students looked around at each other in relief. Platz was a terrible planet for females to live on.

General Lyric looked up at the changing colors of the sky as the day turned into evening. "If there's nothing else, we'll get started."

She put them through two grueling hours of the most demanding exercises they'd ever had in their lifespans. Fawn thought she never wanted to see another sit-up or pull-up ever again. By the time training ended, she could barely pull herself off the ground. Hadna reached down and lifted her to her feet.

The general stood with her hands on her hips, facing the students.

"We'll do intense body mechanics training for a month before you pick up a weapon. Carrying around heavy weapons all day requires peak physical strength."

Her mouth twitched. "Which, at the moment, none of you have."

Fawn groaned. Every muscle in her body ached—even in places she hadn't known she had muscles.

General Lyric grinned at them proudly. Fawn thought she was truly enjoying torturing them.

"Once I build some muscle on you, then we'll begin with the mock fighting. I intend to make you unstoppable. Now line up and get ready for bedtime. You'll be training with me at the end of every week until your time here is up."

Her low, husky voice sent pinpricks into Fawn's belly. "And, students, I don't intend to make it easy on you."

Fawn's heart flip-flopped in her chest. Slowly, she, Hadna, and the other students made their way to the bed chamber. It was going to be a long two years.

The time had come for them to begin training with weapons. While her peers were excited, Fawn found herself wanting the week to go slowly. She wasn't looking forward to training with General Lyric.

While she admired the changes her body had undergone, she didn't like the methods used to condition it. Not only did the general push the students to the limit, she had the dining staff monitor their food intake—no more free choices in what they ate.

The students' meals consisted of lean proteins, lots of vegetables—raw and cooked—and only fruit for dessert and snacks. Since protein was essential for building lean muscle, they could indulge in as much cheese and milk as they wanted.

Dora Reese took pity on them and added crustless cheesecakes to the evening menu. Due to her kindness, Fawn looked forward to the evening snack every night. Unlike Humans, dairy didn't cause them to gain weight and was essential to maintaining healthy bones, hair, and teeth.

Before getting ready for class, Fawn pivoted in the mirror, admiring her new body. Her stomach, taut with a six pack, sculpted arms, thighs, and calves, looked foreign to her. She no longer dreaded running—she found she could keep up with the best runners. Their trainer was waiting for them on the field. Fawn wondered if she enjoyed doing anything other than fighting. She doubted it.

"Good afternoon," said General Lyric. "Welcome to weapons training. Begin your warm-up and I'll get the gear out."

After the warm-up, a familiar dread crept over Fawn. She hoped the general wouldn't call on her to be first. She was wrong.

"Fawn? Grab a sword and let's go," ordered General Lyric. "Grab it the way I showed you and get a grip on your stance.

True ability isn't how well you hold a sword or even how fast you wield it. It's keeping balance between your feet and the hand holding your weapon. If your feet are unsteady, everything goes downhill."

She tapped the soft grass with her foot. "We don't always get to have nice ground like this. There are many times we fight sliding around in blood, brains, and entrails. Keeping your feet steady is crucial to staying ahead of your opponent. Now let's begin. When I swing, you counter."

Fawn thought she'd faint when the general's large sword whizzed by her face. Immediately, she brought up her sword. General Lyric knocked it out of her hand.

"Your mind is elsewhere," she admonished. "It needs to be here," she said, pointing two fingers into her eyes. "Concentrate and focus on me. When you're fighting, you can't afford to let fear conquer you."

She nodded toward Fawn's sword. "Pick it up and try again."

Fawn did as instructed, but no matter how hard she tried, she wasn't able to best the general. After the thirteenth time her sword fell, she began to get angry. Her father's voice screamed in her head.

You're so stupid! Can't you do anything right, Fawn?

Fawn snarled at the unseen figure in her head.

Pick it up, you dolt!

General Lyric frowned. "Fawn? What's the matter? Go on and pick up your sword. I'm not letting you sit until I'm confident you can hold onto it without dropping it. Pick it up."

Pick it up, screamed her father's voice. *Pick it up so everyone can see how worthless you are*!

Fawn retrieved the sword and looked at it. An image of her father's face appeared in the shiny reflection. A strange feeling came over her that she couldn't describe. Before she knew it, she lunged at the general. General Lyric, caught off guard, hadn't had time to defend herself before Fawn knocked the sword out of her hand. Hadna and the others gasped.

"I didn't give the call to start yet, Fawn," said General Lyric. "That was good, but please wait for my instruction."

She turned her back to retrieve the fallen sword as white-hot anger surged within Fawn. She lunged at the general with hatred burning in her eyes.

"Nooooo," screamed her classmates.

"Student 925!" shouted a voice.

General Lyric turned around just in time to see Fawn coming for her before she connected a solid punch to her jaw, sending Fawn flying toward the ground. Fawn thought she saw stars dancing around above her just before she passed out.

W hen Fawn came to, she found herself staring up at General Lyric's bewildered expression.

"I'm going to kill you, Father," she muttered.

General Lyric reached down and pulled her to her feet.
A WomanForm of medium height with a curvaceous figure
sauntered over to where they stood. Fawn looked at her and
would've fallen to her knees were it not for the general's firm
grip.

"I guess you should thank Dora Reese, General Lyric," she
said. "Had I not stopped by to get Queen Revari's pie, you'd be
dead right now."

General Legend's impertinent gaze bore into Fawn. "Student
925, no matter how much we may despise a fellow Sister,
backstabbing is considered the lowest form of dishonor. Now,
what did General Lyric do to make you so angry?"

Fawn struggled to connect her muddled thoughts. It hadn't
been the general's face she'd seen, it was—

"Nothing," said Fawn. "General Lyric hasn't done anything
to me."

General Legend raised a perfectly arched eyebrow. "Then why
did you try to kill her?"

"I didn't!" insisted Fawn. "I didn't try to kill her—it was my
father! I wanted to kill my father!"

General Lyric and General Legend shared a look.

"I see," said General Legend slowly. "There's no doubt you've
had some trauma, but listen to me very carefully. We've all had
our problems with MaleForms. The trick is to not allow them to
ruin our progress."

Her golden eyes scanned Fawn's face. "When you're on this
field with her, pay close attention to her face. You're training

with a general, not your pitiful excuse for a FatherForm. Same goes with me. If you ever try a move like that on me in training, I'll cut your head off and send it to him in pieces. Do you understand?"

"Yes, ma'm," whispered Fawn.

"It's General Legend. It's easy to remember," she said, tossing General Lyric a teasing look. "I'm the prettier one."

General Lyric rolled her eyes toward the Heavens when General Legend winked at her and turned around.

"You owe me one, General Lyric," she tossed over her shoulder.

"I'm aware," said General Lyric.

Turning to Fawn, she placed both hands on her shoulders.

"Fawn, I'm going to teach you to channel your anger. You're no good to anyone if you can't keep a cool head on the battlefield."

"I'm so sorry, General Lyric," sobbed Fawn. "I just saw him and I—"

"It's alright. I've monitored you long enough to know it wasn't me you came for. Still, I agree with what General Legend said. If you don't deal with the anger, it'll ruin your life. You're a top student, and we want to keep you here. Let us help you. Alright?"

Fawn wiped her eyes. "Yes, General. Again, I'm sorry, and thank you for helping me."

General Lyric patted her shoulder. "Good. Now, let's try this again. And this time, wait for my signal."

Chapter 7

F or months, the students tried their best to take the general
down. Eventually, the years flew by. Fawn understood why
Queen Vivant had chosen General Lyric to lead her army—she
was born to be a warrior. On the last day of training, Fawn
looked down at a grinning General Lyric sitting flat on her
behind.

"You finally did it, Fawn. You relieved me of my sword."

Instead of being proud of herself, Fawn started wailing.

General Lyric frowned. "What on Platirius are you crying
about? You passed the training!"

Fawn extended her hand to the general, who took it and
jumped nimbly to her feet. She laughed and gently nudged
Fawn's shoulder. "What are you going on about, Student 925?"

Fawn sniffed. "I don't want to leave you."

It was true. She didn't. She had grown to respect General Lyric
more than she realized. She was the big sister she'd never had. All
of the students felt that way. She was tough, yet never made the
students feel as if they were incompetent or stupid.

She'd worked hard to ensure they reached their potential.
The students knew they had succeeded because she cared about

them. Her warm compassion and fighting spirit were more than they had expected.

General Lyric's look was pensive. "Well, if the Milan of Honor deems it, you'll be back here with us in no time. Remember what I told you about channeling your anger. Don't let it spiral out of control. If you lose yourself, you'll lose everything."

General Lyric stuck out her hand. Fawn shook it with enthusiasm.

"You'll do well, Fawn. No matter where you go, you'll always have Sisters here cheering you on."

Tears of joy sprang in Fawn's eyes. "I'll never forget you, General Lyric."

General Lyric flashed a rare, stunning smile. "I'll hold you to that."

She turned to the students and clapped her hands. "You've gone above and beyond to prove you're the best and the brightest young females. I'm very proud to say you've finished your physical examinations with flying colors. You'll wrap up with Captain TamRi and get ready for the next leg of your journey. Collect the gear and line up."

The students hurried to grab all the weapons, armor, and supplies to take them to the sanitizing station in the back of the instruction chamber.

G eneral Lyric stood next to Captain TamRi.

"When you go to Revani, remember everything I taught you. General Legend agreed to incorporate a few of General Kron's techniques, yet she and I have different mindsets. I implore you to stay true to yourselves on Revani. The Vivacians and Revaltians are two sides of a coin. Flip carefully. Where you land will determine your destiny."

Every student's eyes filled with tears when they saluted her. She nodded once before departing, leaving them to wonder what awaited them on Revani.

Captain TamRi smiled warmly at her class. "Welcome back, students. All of your belongings have been packed and loaded onto the crafts."

A hushed silence fell over the chamber. The students braced themselves for what was coming next.

"I've transmitted the grades for your final examinations. They'll download by this evening."

Pride swelled within her as she observed the young WomenForms she'd grown attached to. "You've all done amazingly well with everything I've taught you. The years have flown by, and your time with me has come to an end. You're now ready for the next step in your journey. When the chime rings, line up to board the crafts for your trip to Revani."

Tears dropped like rain down the faces of Fawn and her classmates. They'd grown to care about the captain as much as she cared for them.

"Your assigned craft numbers are on your palms. Please board quickly and quietly. I'll be praying for all of you to succeed, but I have a feeling my prayers have already been answered."

She cleared her throat. "Remember to show Colonel Sheila the same respect you demonstrated with me. Platirius and Revani work together as a single unit to provide you with the best education. We expect nothing less than the best from our students. Class is dismissed."

A beautiful WomanForm of medium height stood at the front of the classroom, flanked by General Legend and a gorgeous MaleForm the students couldn't take their eyes off. Fawn noted her raven-black hair and café-au-lait skin tone. Her eyebrows were perfectly arched above almond-shaped brown eyes. Not one hair was out of place and her makeup was expertly applied.

Fawn wondered if it had been applied with a *Shoni*, a hand-held tool that pulled moisture from the air to accentuate makeup looks that lasted until they were removed with skin conditioner. Her red lips coordinated with a red uniform with dozens of highly polished medals. Fawn admired her thigh-high red boots with high heels. She doubted she'd ever come that close to looking like perfection.

"Good morning, class. I'm your instructor, Colonel Sheila. Welcome to Revani, where you'll complete your final years of the ParaNurture physician program. I'm sure Captain TamRi and General Lyric have already given you an excellent foundation. I suggest you hold onto it."

Her dark eyes sliced through the students like a hot knife through butter.

"Your training will become more rigorous until you reach the final examination with me and skilled physical assessments on the battlefield with General Legend."

"Good morning, students. I'm General Legend."

Fawn's breath caught when the general winked at her. "I met you briefly on Platirius. During the week, you'll take lessons in the classroom, but on weekends, you'll train with me from morning until evening."

Fawn stared at the gorgeous, buxom WomanForm in awe. On Platirius, she'd barely glanced at her, but now she noted the general was curvier than General Lyric's tall, lean frame and had a small mole on the right side of her mouth. Her full lips hid perfectly aligned teeth. She audaciously bared much more of her ample cleavage than General Lyric.

Her athletic, muscular thighs were also encased in thigh-high red boots. Her wide, golden eyes were lined with thick lashes, and her honey-brown skin was smooth and blemish-free. Fawn looked down at her lithe physique and frowned.

She'd never had large breasts, and her legs looked like slim branches. She would've given anything to look that confident

JANIUS PAWNS BOOK I

and sexy. Her eyes found a large diamond ring on General Legend's hand.

I wonder who she's married to.

"Hello, students. I'm Gallium Barrios. I'll be teaching you how to make chemical weapons when you're not with Colonel Sheila or General Legend. I'm very pleased to meet all of you."

Fawn's breath caught in her throat. Out of the corner of her eye, she sought the reactions of her classmates. All of them were staring at Gallium as if he had sprouted horns on his head. Domi's mouth had dropped open and stayed open. Fawn knew exactly how she felt.

Gallium's face and muscular physique could stop crafts in mid-Space.

General Legend threw back her head and laughed. "Here we go again," she said, tossing him a saucy wink.

"Don't start," he muttered good-naturedly.

"Yes, well, you just remember where you park your shears, General Barrios," she whispered to him before planting a kiss on his full lips.

Captivated by the couple, the class gasped at the small display of affection.

"Out," he said to her. "We're not here to give the ChildForms that kind of show."

He laughed when she pouted and exited. As his sea-green eyes sought out the young WomenForms, a wave of melancholy flowed through him. They reminded him of his sisters who had perished on Coldarius.

Making a sharp pivot toward Colonel Sheila, he said, "Colonel, send them to me on the second and fourth days for a couple of hours, and I'll return them to you to finish up."

Colonel Sheila nodded at him. "That'll work, Gallium. Thank you."

He nodded at her and the students and smiled.

"I'll see all of you tomorrow. Thank you."

The students melted when he exited.

"Wow, I never thought I'd see any MaleForm that beautiful on Revani," Domi gushed.

A round of laughter followed.

"If I were you, I'd focus on your lessons," said Colonel Sheila. "You'll soon see how skilled General Legend is on the field. Gallium is her husband. You may look, but don't be cute and try anything further. I wouldn't want to get on her bad side."

Domi swallowed hard while the rest of the students quickly sobered. General Legend had an impressive record within the galaxy. Gallium was beautiful, but no MaleForm was worth a severed head.

Domi raised her hand. "Does he have any brothers?"

"He did," said Colonel Sheila.

Domi frowned. "What happened to him?"

Colonel Sheila looked her dead in the eye. "He was beheaded by Queen Revari."

Unmoved by their shocked expressions, she smiled at them.

"I thank The One that it's finally quiet. Let's get started. Although your classes are combined, the research students have been given a special project to work on—to discover a cure for a disease that was brought to us by a Human. It is called Alzheimer's disease. As of now, it has affected only one Being. We intend to keep it that way."

She waved her hand to lower the instruction chamber's lighting.

"The Humans have no cure for Alzheimer's disease, but that's no surprise. Although their governments discovered the cure for cancer and AIDS decades ago, they've been selfishly hoarding the cures for many of their diseases. The longer they keep each other dependent on pharmaceuticals, the more money they make. It's sheer avarice."

An amused smile brightened her face. "Years ago, we made a killing selling Allebri to Humans—literally and financially."

Bracing her arms on the large desk, she said, "We found the cure for these diseases three thousand years before Humans. However, Alzheimer's wasn't something that piqued our interest until now."

She walked to a large window and pointed to a chamber across the courtyard. "Human scientists are housed there. When they landed on Revani by accident, they weren't allowed to leave. They'll remain here until we discover a cure for Alzheimer's."

"Will we be working closely with them?" asked Hadna. "Will we get to speak to them?"

Colonel Sheila's eyes took on a sinister gleam. "Communication isn't necessary to learn what they know."

She waved her hand in the air again. Immediately, images of six Human males and one female suspended in the air appeared. Dozens of wires, small lights, and electrodes were attached to their heads. They appeared to be asleep until one of the flashing lights sounded, causing one of them to cry out.

"They're connected to brain scanners. They're used to assimilate all of their knowledge into our systems. Once that's over, their usefulness wears out."

"And then they go home?" asked Domi.

"No Human leaves Revani alive," said Colonel Sheila firmly. "We don't allow Humans to roam our planet as if they own it."

Her tone left no room for argument.

"You may begin copying your notes now. On Earth, Alzheimer's is the leading cause of dementia in older Humans. In the brain, Alzheimer's is marked by harmful clumps called plaques, tangled fibers known as neurofibrillary tangles, and the loss of brain cells. Memory loss is the first sign of deterioration within the brain, followed by severe deficits in behavior and cognition."

She waved her hand again. The images of the Human scientists were replaced by dozens of mice held within clear containers.

"Transgenic mice are trained to replicate certain aspects of Alzheimer's. Amyloid is a protein that plays a major role in its development. Now, the mice don't provide a mirror image of what transpires in the Human body. However, they've been effective in learning the destructive effects of amyloid. A valuable clue we've taken from Human scientists is how to leverage the Human immune system."

An image materialized in the air after she snapped her fingers.

"To provide a clear picture of how Alzheimer's affects the brain, Human symptoms need to be duplicated in mice via genetic changes linked to the disease. So how did we do it? We induced deposits of beta-amyloid, a toxic protein. This caused damage to brain cells and led to changes in behavior in the mice."

Domi furrowed her nose.

"These are your subjects," said Colonel Sheila.

Fawn suppressed the urge to giggle at Domi's defeated expression. Domi hated mice. Although they'd been warned not to get on General Legend's bad side, Fawn's intuition told her not to make Colonel Sheila angry either.

"This is Human research, so I'd like you to take it with a grain of salt. We don't copy Humans. They wouldn't have survived this long had we not taught the ancient civilizations many of the skills they needed to survive."

The lecture continued for a couple more hours before Colonel Sheila said, "Class is dismissed for lunch. Please report to the dining chamber and return to the classroom within one hour sharp."

I t was six months before they found the cure.

"I know what we need to do," said Kaddah, a reticent research student. "Look here," she said, tapping a sterile rod on a small section of a mouse's brain on a screen.

"I eliminated the amyloid protein completely and discovered a new approach. Unlike the Humans, whose brains control them, we control ours. We used the Human scientists as our control group and a group of Beings imprisoned in the confinement chamber as our experimental group."

Kaddah's clear brown eyes danced with excitement.

"We subjected the experimental group to rigorous cognitive behavioral therapy sessions and learned we can produce a toxin called *Pherosome* that kills off the plaque and neurofibrillary tangles. *Pherosome* has a side effect—it causes Beings to become extremely sexually aroused."

Kaddah clapped her hands together. "Yet, during the period where *Pherosome is produced, they latch on to the specific proteins within the brain, replicating* whatever structure is needed to function properly, while simultaneously killing off the toxic bits. The replica is a new part of the body that is fully functioning, leaving no trace that the brain was ever affected by Alzheimer's."

She bit her lip. "*Pherosome* only works in Beings' brains. Once we introduced them to Human DNA, they took over their brains completely, wiping out their memories and entire identity. *Pherosome* created an entirely different persona!"

Kaddah grinned at her classmates, truly delighted with her discovery.

"Here's the sweet spot. *Pherosome* travels from Human to Human through copulation."

She noted Fawn's doubtful look.

"I'm telling you, it can. A criminal Being broke free of the straps and forcefully copulated with the female scientist before we had a chance to introduce *Pherosome* intravenously."

She punched data into the TranScreen. "Take a look at her brain."

Domi gasped. "It looks just like the others!"

"Precisely," said Kaddah smugly.

Irritated by her show of arrogance, Domi frowned at Kaddah. "But how did he get to her to violate her? They were in separate cubes and we weren't given permission to experiment on them."

Kaddah's unhinged gaze bordered on frightening. "They didn't say we couldn't use the Human specimens either. It's not my responsibility to keep them safe as long as they deliver the answers we need."

Turning off the TranScreen, she said, "Now, we know Beings have been going to Earth for missions for millions of years, but what if Queen Revari wanted to return the Humans fully instilled with our knowledge? We've found a way to take over the Human species permanently!"

"And have the wrath of The One fall down on all of us?"

They all turned around to meet Colonel Sheila's enraged face.

"I told you to find a way to eliminate Alzheimer's. I never instructed you to make decisions above your pay grade."

Kaddah visibly trembled as the colonel approached her.

"Instructor Sheila, I—"

"It's Colonel Sheila," she interrupted. "This is Revani. And here, no one goes over the authority of Queen Revari."

She reached down and grabbed Kaddah by the collar. "Do you think you're smarter than everyone here, including our queen?"

"N-no, Colonel Sheila! I was just—"

"Showing off," said Colonel Sheila. "You could've stopped with combining the genetically altered cells of the Beings with *Pherosome*. That would've been enough."

Suddenly, it dawned on all of the students. Kaddah looked at her in disbelief. "You mean...you already had the cure?"

Colonel Sheila's lips curled into a menacing smile. "Of course. Did you really think we needed a bunch of ChildForms to discover what we already know? You've gone above and beyond, Student 507. Too bad all that got you was a trip to the confinement chamber."

"For what?" choked Kaddah.

"Not that I need to answer to you, but it gives me so much pleasure to see you finally knocked off your self-absorbed pedestal. Let me ask you something. Did you have Queen Revari's permission to use her Human specimens for anything other than finding a cure?"

Kaddah blinked. "No," she squeaked. "I thought I'd help her."

"You, a student, help the greatest ruler in the entire galaxy? Are you that arrogant you think she needs your help?"

Laughing in her face, she let go of her collar and nodded to two Revaltian soldiers. "Lock her down well. Queen Revari will decide what's to be done with her."

Terrified, Kaddah shrank back from the Revaltian soldiers. They picked her up as if she weighed less than a bag of candy and dragged her out of the research chamber.

Colonel Sheila turned her ominous smile on the rest of the students. "The little show is over. I want this research chamber to be spotless. Then collect your things and report to your bed chambers. If one of you even thinks of pulling a stunt like that again, you'll be locked up so fast, you won't know what hit you. You're here to learn. Not to advance yourselves over us."

Her deep black eyes raked over them. "Never bite the hand that feeds you. It might just snap your neck. Class is dismissed."

Fawn slid across the ground for the sixth time. General Legend had been tossing her and the other students across the field all evening. She was tired, sore, hungry, and felt extremely dispirited. As for General Legend, she hadn't broken a sweat.

"Get up, Fawn. Last I checked, the grass didn't give its hand in marriage."

It was a good joke, but none of the students laughed. They all knew exactly how Fawn felt. They'd trained for over a year, but no matter how hard they tried, none of them had managed to defeat the general. Her beauty had fooled them.

General Legend was an exceptional fighter. Unlike General Lyric, whose fighting skills were upfront and honest, she thrived on exploiting her opponents' weaknesses.

The general hadn't forgotten Fawn's weak spot—her father. Whenever she could, she goaded Fawn by calling her "Father's Little Pet." It enraged Fawn beyond reason. The angrier she became, the harder she fought, which ultimately led to her falling hard at the general's feet.

"Come on, Father's Little Pet. What's the matter? Can't do anything without your rich FatherForm? How will you be a better physician than him if you can't even defend yourself?"

That did it. Fawn's light brown eyes shot to the general's golden ones. She slowly got to her feet and picked up her weapon. Forcing herself to breathe slowly and evenly, she said, "I'm ready, General Legend."

General Legend flashed her beautiful smile. "It took you long enough!"

When she advanced, Fawn quickly blocked a blow. The general was light on her feet and even faster with her hands. If Fawn didn't feel a cut to her uniform, it was a sharp blow to her chest or a hard tug on her hair. General Legend abhorred striking students in the face.

"No need for WomenForms to go around looking like busted-up MaleForms unless they have to," she'd informed the students on the first day of training.

"So against all odds, protect your faces when you see my hands coming and protect them even when you don't. MaleForms love to go for our eyes. If we can't see them, they think we're helpless. During the final days leading up to the end of the program, I'll teach you to fight blindfolded."

And she had. Unfortunately, the students' fighting techniques hadn't improved. She fought too hard and much too dirty. Truthfully, none of them had the heart to follow her tricks. General Lyric had unknowingly conditioned them to fight fairly.

But now, Fawn felt herself forgetting all that she'd promised General Lyric. The urge to defeat General Legend was stronger than any moral code she'd held before.

Before she knew it, she said, "Yes, my father is wealthy, but I hear yours wasn't. No matter how well you fight, you'll always be a poor, dirty commoner!"

The students gaped at Fawn, who clasped her hand over her mouth.

Where in the galaxy had that come from?

She'd never looked down her nose at any Being before. General Legend smiled craftily. Unbeknownst to Fawn and her classmates, the Milan of Honor awakened, glowing softly under the stars.

"Well, you rich little twit, let's see you beat this poor, dirty general!"

They clashed swords, back and forth, for what seemed like hours. Neither WomanForm wanted to give the other the slightest advantage. When she placed another cut on her thigh, Fawn screamed in rage.

She charged at the general with a burst of energy she hadn't known was left. In the end, it was for naught. General Legend knocked her sword out of her hand, grabbed her by the hair, and forced her to kneel.

"You're a good fighter, Fawn," she said, placing her long sword under her neck. The students held their breath as she leaned down to peer into Fawn's face.

"But you'll never be as good as me!" She yanked on her hair. "Now say you surrender."

Fawn snarled. "Never, you buxom whore!"

Hadna nearly fainted, and Domi's mouth dropped for the third time since practice began.

General Legend cocked her head. "What did you say to me?"

"I said NEVER, YOU BUXOM WHORE!" shouted Fawn.

She screamed when General Legend pulled harder on her mass of thick, tight curls.

"Surrender or I'll make you bald here and now!" shouted General Legend.

"Do it!" spat Fawn.

General Legend raised her sword and chopped off all of Fawn's wavy, reddish-brown locks. When she was done, Fawn's smooth head resembled a young MaleForm's.

Domi stared at Fawn in shock. Hadna sobbed openly.

"If you become a Revaltian, you'll be under my command. When your general tells you to do something, you do it!"

"You're not my general yet," said Fawn through angry tears. "You may have beaten me, but you'll never make me admit defeat!"

"I can change that," said a cocky voice.

Colonel Angela came up behind Fawn and placed her foot on the back of her head, pushing her face into the ground. Hadna held her face in her hands, silently crying out for Fawn to surrender. Colonel Angela let her foot up just enough so Fawn could get air into her lungs again.

"You have balls of fire, don't you, JanIan?" Hunkering down to Fawn, she said, "But you're not on JanIus. This is Revani."

She pointed to General Legend. "She controls this army. You don't think we'll let you get away with thinking you're on our level, do you?"

Still sprawled on her stomach, Fawn turned her head to look up into the colonel's dark eyes. She couldn't utter a sound.

Colonel Angela rose and stepped on the side of her head. "Did you hear me, JanIan? I asked a question."

Silence.

Colonel Angela looked at General Legend. Throwing back her head and laughing, she said, "Oh! We have a live one here, General! She thinks she's tough!"

General Legend observed Fawn with pity. "Yes, she does. I wonder what we'll do with her?" she asked mockingly.

Colonel Angela's eyes narrowed to slits. "We're gonna break her," she promised.

General Legend summoned sixteen troops out onto the field. Eight flanked on Fawn's right and left side.

"I want you to think very carefully about what you're doing," she said to Fawn. "Either you surrender right now, or we're going to beat the hell out of you until you do."

"Surrender, Fawn," whispered Hadna. "Surrender!"

But Fawn wouldn't. She glared up at General Legend and spat on the ground.

General Legend smiled at her, but it didn't meet the frostiness in her eyes.

"As you wish, JanIan," she said softly. "I'm going to join my sister for supper."

Tossing her sword to a student to clean, she said, "Have fun."

Her hips swayed sassily as she turned her back on Fawn and left her to her fate.

"Hoist her up!" commanded Colonel Angela.

The Revaltians lifted Fawn roughly to her feet. Colonel Angela put her finger in the center of Fawn's forehead. "You're mine now, JanIan."

The Revaltians took turns pummeling Fawn. After about an hour had passed, her body was so sore that she could barely move.

Gallium came rushing out of a craft from JanIus. "What on Revani is going on here?" he shouted. "You're going to kill her!"

Colonel Angela pointed at him. "This is Revaltian business! It doesn't concern you!"

"She's not a Revaltian, she's a student! And an unskilled fighter at that! If you kill her, what does that prove?"

Colonel Angela got in his face. "You are not a Revaltian!" she said through clenched teeth. "This doesn't concern *you*, so stay out of it!"

Gallium didn't flinch. "No! I'm no Revaltian, but I never stopped being a general! And I don't take orders from you, Colonel!" shouted Gallium.

"And I don't listen to filthy MaleForms!" Sticking a finger in his chest, she said, "On what planet are you a general?" asked Colonel Angela.

She stepped back when a vein began moving across his chest toward her finger.

"Colonel Angela and Gallium!" a low, husky voice said.

Immediately, Gallium and Colonel Angela pivoted and saluted the figure standing on the balcony.

Chapter 8

"The dining staff has prepared an excellent meal of sea bass pan-fried in butter, seasoning, and lemon. My mouth is watering for the courgettes and a mélange of quinoa, bell pepper, mushroom, and pak choi with rice."

Red manicured nails drummed against the coolness of the ruby structure. "But, before I could sample a bite, I heard yelling and screaming beyond my halls. Who wants to be the first to tell me why?"

Colonel Angela bowed. "Queen Revari, we're teaching this student a lesson, but Gallium is interfering in our business! He's not a Revaltian nor is he in charge of us—General Legend is."

"I'm well aware of who the general of my army is," said Queen Revari. "Was it not I who appointed her, Colonel?"

Colonel Angela bowed again. "Yes, My Queen."

Queen Revari's cool gaze scanned the students until she reached Fawn sprawled out on the ground.

"Student 925," she called. "If you think you're too tough to surrender, I'll gladly come down there and make you. But if I have to leave my beautiful meal, your head is as good as severed. Have I been heard?"

Her voice never rose, but the deadly promise ringing in her tone terrified Fawn. On wobbly knees, she tried to rise to her feet and was hoisted up by two Revaltians.

"I—I already surrendered, Your-Your Highness," she stammered, swaying from left to right.

The Revaltians allowed her to fall face-first into the ground.

Queen Revari's eyes shifted to Colonel Angela. "Is this true?"

"Yes, but I didn't like having to wait nearly an hour to hear it," Colonel Angela said.

"Because you're sadistic," muttered Gallium.

"And you're a lying, sneaky MaleForm," hissed Colonel Angela.

"I've never known Gallium to lie," said Queen Revari. Her eyes found his. "Why is she calling you a liar?"

"She doesn't believe that I'm a general!" he said fiercely.

Raising an eyebrow, Queen Revari leaned forward on the balcony. "Oh? Who appointed you?"

So it's true, thought Gallium. *She doesn't remember all of her past.*

At one time, he and Queen Revari had shared a close connection, but after spending several long years in the Chamber of Despair, her memories were sparse. Gallium guessed it was due to suffering from severe depression.

No one understood her better than he. King Dubian had made her ChildForm years unbearable when he or General Legend weren't around to protect her. He'd purposely sent them to Earth to unleash his fury on her.

Losing her husband and her son was the final act that broke her. Since she'd refused to allow Queen Vivant to heal her, erasing parts of her mind like a program was an unexpected consequence of the years of trauma inflicted on her.

He met her eyes. "Your mother," he said softly.

"Queen Dellah appointed me general of her army after we defeated the Kikhanians. She was carrying you at the time. She saw the whole thing from a high window, much like the one you're watching from now. She trained us to fight with honor, not like this," he said, gesturing to Fawn's crumpled form.

Everyone stood still except Gallium, who furiously clenched and unclenched his fists.

"I understand Colonel Angela has a distinctive way of fighting, but beating this ChildForm almost to death unnerved me. If she's already surrendered, where's the honor in continuing to beat her so mercilessly?"

The night was silent as everyone waited with bated breath to hear what Queen Revari would say. Queen Dellah was a touchy subject. No one except Gallium and Queen Vivant dared to mention her mother in her presence. It was the only time she showed the slightest bit of vulnerability.

"Mother," she whispered. Raising her head, she faced her soldiers and the students. "What my mother decreed will stand. However, General Barrios, no MaleForm will ever have a position of leadership in my army. I hope you'll accept being my confidant and my SecondFather instead. I love you dearly, but you must never interfere in Revaltian business again. Have I been heard?"

Gallium's heart soared. She hadn't expressed affection for him since she was a young ChildForm.

There must be some memories of me left if she thinks of me as a FatherForm.

Having no idea how important he was to her until just then, he blinked back tears. "Yes, Your Highness."

"Colonel Angela, we may fight dirty at times, but not with female students. We need to ensure we're doing everything the right way—the way Queen Dellah would've wanted. I don't want to do anything to shame my mother's memory. Have I been heard?"

Colonel Angela saluted her again. "Yes, Your Highness."

"Are there any records left of her trainings, Gallium?" asked Queen Revari.

"No," he said. "Everything was destroyed on Coldarius. But it's all still in my head."

"Good, then you'll share it with me and we'll pass it on to General Legend to share with my Revaltians."

Her silver eyes scanned Fawn's crumpled form once more. "Now, I'm hungry. Get that ChildForm off the ground and send the rest to their chambers for supper and bed. General Barrios, will you please join me and General Legend? I had the dining staff prepare a fat pheasant with herbed dressing for you."

Gallium smiled at her. "Yes, My Queen."

It took weeks for Fawn to recover from her injuries. Over time, her tenacity and bravery earned the respect of the Revaltians—even Colonel Angela. General Legend pinned medals on the students when the training had come to an end.

She was still undefeated, but the students didn't mind. They were proud they'd learned to fight from the only female generals in the galaxy. Gallium's final class was also bittersweet. He'd thoroughly enjoyed sharing his love of plants with the students.

"I'm so proud of all of you for listening and doing well on your exams. Callidut is my invention and it's the deadliest I've fashioned so far. I've shown you what to mix with it and what not to. It can be used to heal or destroy Beings."

Raising a finger in the air, he said, "It's only to be used in acts of war, and only with Queen Revari's permission. Only Revani has Callidut. Since I make it by special order, you won't find it on any of the other planets."

He paused. "And it's banned on Platirius."

His revelation surprised the students, but he didn't elaborate.

"I don't need to remind you that if you're caught mixing substances or using them, the penalty is death. It doesn't matter what planet you're assigned to. Every surveillance team has strict orders to be on the alert for toxic substances."

He wiped his eyes and sighed. It was very difficult to talk about Dr. Barrios, but he felt it was important for the students to understand how destructive addiction could be.

"My brother was a doctor. He was sent to Earth for many missions for our former ruler, King Carlomon. The horrors he witnessed were too much for him to bear…"

The students patiently waited for him to collect himself.

"He fell into addiction. I had no idea he'd been using the Callidut to cope with anxiety and depression. If I had, I would've made sure he received the help he needed. In the end, it destroyed him."

Fawn watched as he struggled not to show emotion in front of them. "I blame myself. Had I not invented Callidut, maybe he'd still be here with me. I realize now he was too focused on his pain to understand how losing the last surviving member of my family would affect me."

He jumped down from the desk and stood in the middle of the research chamber.

"That's the point I want to bring home. Toxic substances don't just hurt you—they destroy everyone around you—family, friends, even strangers. I've taught you to protect your lives, not destroy them. Promise me you'll remember that."

He smiled when the students murmured their agreement. "That's all I have for you. I'd say you're ready for the final leg of the program. You'll be receiving your final grades tomorrow just in time for the graduation ceremony and feast."

Domi raised her hand. "And we'll find out where we'll be stationed too, right, Gallium?"

Gallium nodded. "Yes, Domi. Very soon, you'll learn where you'll be stationed." He raised his hands in the air. "I can't give you any clues. You'll have to find out tomorrow evening."

He laughed at their good-natured groans. He'd truly miss them. They were a good bunch of ChildForms. He only hoped they'd adhere to everything they'd been taught—especially the student the queens were interested in. She had no idea what she'd signed up for. That worried him. Immensely.

"She's almost completed the program. Will you send her back to JanIus once it's over?"

She stretched her legs out on the plush mattress and stared up at the stars through the transparent ceiling. "Since when do I answer to you? I own you and your planet. Never question me, Leighton."

He bit his lip. Angering her was the last thing he wanted to do. "Forgive me. I'm kind of in the dark is all. Prince Justin is on JanIus and he has no clue I know who he really is. If the young WomanForm returns, things might get complicated."

His eyes roamed over her large, firm breasts, making him lick his lips in anticipation of another round of lovemaking.

Looking deeply into his sparkling periwinkle eyes, she said, "If things become complicated, I'll have to uncomplicate them by slicing your throat. It would be wise not to defy me, Leighton. I have plans for Prince Justin and the student. Don't get in my way."

"You know I'd never do anything to hurt you. I love you!"

He stifled a groan when she pinched his taut nipple between her fingertips. "Do you ever tire of saying such foolish things? Maybe I can find a better use for your tongue, yes?" she said, lying on her back.

Smiling eagerly, he leaned his muscular physique closer to her, positioning his head between her thighs.

"Your wish is my command."

She dug the heel of her boot into his thigh. Her eyes rolled back in her head when he found the right spot. "Don't speak anymore unless I want you to."

The Milan of Honor stood at the center of the beautifully decorated recreation chamber. Rows of heavy tables made of solid gold were covered in gilded ruby and gold silk tablecloths made by Marcia Blight, Queen Dellah's seamstress and personal fashion consultant. Veteran dining staff Dora Reese and Sandi Childler teamed up with Revani's dining staff to prepare the celebration feast.

Gallium had created beautiful centerpieces of elaborate red roses, white tulips, lilies, and gold hydrangeas surrounding busts carved from diamonds. Each one captured Queen Dellah's radiant beauty in magnificent poses, materialized from his memories as a soldier.

On Queen Revari and Queen Vivant's table sat a bust of their mother—pregnant with the younger queen. Queen Vivant, only seven summers, stood at her side, her small hand resting on her protruding belly. They both stared straight ahead, smiling and happy. Gallium's precious glimpses of the past had made even the sternest of soldiers wipe a tear from their eye—even Colonel Angela.

The students' eyes were as large as the platters that held the endless, mouthwatering recipes that had graced the tables of the royal families for generations. Charcuterie boards with smoked meats and cheeses sat alongside expertly crafted crudité platters.

Plump chickens roasted with lemons, garlic, spices, thyme, and rosemary waited in long, platinum trays beside thick venison and beef roasts swimming in gravy with celery, carrots, and onions. The aroma of thick, medium-rare steaks filled the air. Fawn anticipated sampling fried chicken cylinders and roasted pheasants—ancient Coldarian recipes provided by Gallium.

For seafood lovers, ribbons of steam rose above platters of sea bass, trout, candied salmon bites, jumbo shrimp, bay scallops, sea scallops, lobster tails, and stuffed crab. Ruby and gold pans of mashed potatoes, cubed potatoes roasted with garlic and onions, honeyed sweet potatoes, fried sweet corn, corn pudding, and candied carrots sat on tables opposite cold vegetable and fruit salads.

Domi, a pasta lover, was excited to see cavatappi in a decadent sauce made with four cheeses, lemon fusilli with peas, and pappardelle with shitake mushrooms in a creamy white wine sauce. Steaming white and purple rice sat next to beef tips and gravy.

Revani's dining staff added many of Queen Revari's favorites—pernil, arroz con pollo—rice with chicken, tostones—fried plantains, arroz con gandules—rice, pork, and pigeon peas seasoned with sofrito, moros y cristianos—black beans and rice, lechon asado—roasted pork, pastelitos, and picadillo—ground beef with capers and olives.

Fawn had never seen so much food in her lifespan. Hadna gleefully brought her attention to the dessert tables. Their eyes widened at dozens of chocolate, spice, orange, and honey lemon cakes.

Hadna's mouth watered for the Cuban flan—a thick, rich, custard-style dessert with a caramelized topping. There were also peach, apple, blueberry, and cherry pies with flaky crusts, peach and apple cobblers, and wide crystal containers filled with trifle.

Champagne, PotterBerry, and ChayBray wines were reserved for the AdultForms, while the students spied an impressive selection of sweet PotterBerry juice, lemonade, and sun tea flowing from large, sparkling crystal containers.

Everything was so beautifully decorated that Fawn felt as if she were a princess. She thought she'd die when Princess Tarah asked her, Hadna, and Domi to sit at their table with the queens and members of the Instruction Council. Fawn happily sat next to Captain TamRi, who squeezed her arm with pride.

Excitement buzzed in the air. They had successfully completed the ParaNurture and Researcher programs, passing their examinations with flying colors. Fawn spotted a line of ParentForms entering the chamber and was relieved when hers were escorted to the back to be seated.

She pointedly ignored her mother waving to her before her father's fierce scowl quickly silenced her. He quickly checked himself, looking around the room to see if he had caught anyone's attention. Queen Revari's scathing glare had been trained on him since he entered.

While Fawn wasn't surprised he'd earned the queen's ire, she did a double take at the frosty gaze Queen Vivant directed his way. She hadn't realized she knew of her father.

She hoped he'd be on his best behavior. The last thing she wanted was to end up embarrassed by his antics. She watched Queen Revari whisper something in Gallium's ear, and he got up and strolled over to her father.

When he leaned down and whispered something in his ear, Dr. Azini stiffened. Gallium stared him down for a few seconds until he wilted under his glare. He'd just been put on notice. If he showed the slightest sign of disrespect, he'd be dealt with. Fawn wished Gallium could be her surrogate FatherForm too.

Laughter filled the chamber as royalty, leaders, students, and their families broke bread together under one roof. Fawn tried to hold back tears when Hadna and Domi's parents cheered loudly for them as their names were called to accept their awards. Hand in hand, they stood in front of the Milan of Honor.

Hadna held her breath and stepped forward. Immediately, the stone glowed platinum! She'd be joining the Vivacians! Queen Vivant and General Lyric stood and cheered loudly for their newest member. Overwhelmed by their love and acceptance, Hadna wiped tears of joy from her eyes.

Domi was next. The fierce glow turned black. Domi would be stationed on Onzi, a planet led by King Asa. Domi met the king's chilly gaze with a nod. His gaze drifted to meet the crimson fire glowing in Queen Revari's eyes.

After he inclined his head respectfully toward her, Queen Vivant and Queen Revari shared a look Fawn couldn't decipher. She didn't think the king was pleased to have a WomanForm physician joining his planet.

Her turn was next. Her mother clapped loudly with the others while her father pasted a false smile on his face. Fawn knew he was seething underneath. He'd never wanted her to become anything except a housewife who took orders from a husband.

She accepted the award presented to her by Colonel Sheila and General Legend and saluted them. Their warm smiles made her smile. They were genuinely proud of her.

Shyly, Fawn bowed to Queen Revari and nearly fainted when the queen slightly inclined her head toward her. She was a tiny, muscular WomanForm with silver eyes and dimples that matched her sister's, yet that's where the similarities ended.

Queen Vivant's lithe, lush frame was almost six feet tall. Her skin was several shades lighter than her sister's, and her long, flowing locks were the color of the sun.

Queen Revari's cinnamon hue was complemented by her long, curly, raven-black hair. She had a small mole on her upper lip and one right above her right eye. Both of the queens were absolutely stunning.

Fawn's eyes traveled to the larger-than-life painting of Queen Dellah. While she could easily see the late queen's features in Queen Vivant, Queen Revari bore an uncanny resemblance to their breathtaking mother.

Everyone waited for her to stand before the Milan of Honor. A strange feeling washed over her. At first, she felt hot, then a mysterious power lulled her senses. The stone's rays shone so brightly, they almost blinded her.

At first, they glowed bright white. Fawn thought she heard a cough. Confused, she looked into the crowd and caught the mocking eyes of her father.

Anger bubbled up and flooded through her like a river. Instantly, the colors changed from white to a bright, angry red. Dr. Azini watched his daughter's light brown eyes turn crimson while she stared at him with all the pent-up hatred that had mounted over the years.

Recalling all the beatings he'd subjected her to caused her to release a flood of fury she hadn't realized was there. Someone in the audience gasped. Then another. The stone began trembling under the rage churning within Fawn. Furious whispers flew among the frightened spectators.

General Lyric rose and quickly reached Fawn, placing a firm hand on her shoulder. Immediately, she felt calmer—more at peace. The fiery hues ebbed to a soft red glow. Suddenly, half of the stone changed to violet.

The Revaltians cheered while the stunned spectators clapped. Never in history had the Milan of Honor displayed different colors.

What does it mean? thought Fawn.

Queen Revari smiled. "We have a Revaltian who's headed for JanIus!"

Fawn's heart sank.

I'm going to take orders from him?

A secretive smile played on Queen Revari's lips. "You may return to your seat, Fawn."

Dutifully, Fawn followed her order. Queen Revari approached Queen Vivant and stood by her side.

"My sister and I would like to thank everyone who attended the graduation ceremony to support our students tonight. Our first ParaNurture and Galactic Researcher program was a success. I know our mother, Queen Dellah, is extremely proud of us for doing this in her honor," said Queen Revari.

Queen Vivant was next. "We're very proud of all our students and are happy to supply you with the trained professionals your planet so desperately needs. A few of our soldiers will escort everyone out except for the MaleForm physicians who lead medical chambers and private practices. We need to discuss the final plans for receiving your new ParaNurture physicians. Thank you all for coming."

Everyone stood and bowed to the queens before exiting the recreation chamber.

M rs. Corral stood in front of Queen Revari in her spacious meeting chamber. She marveled at the golden statues of pumas, panthers, tigers, and lionesses that complemented the lavish décor. The queen's BrainStaffs, displayed in a luxurious ruby cube, glowed softly.

Queen Revari sat at the massive desk inlaid with diamonds and rubies. Her eyes scanned the instructor's comfortable heels and modest evening gown.

"No need to sit, Mrs. Corral, this won't take long."

Mrs. Corral mimicked her in raising her palm. She nearly fainted when she reviewed the sum that the queen transmitted to her.

"This is for your role in getting the JanIan student signed up for the program."

Speechless, Mrs. Corral bowed to her. "Thank you, Your Majesty!"

Queen Revari tossed her a bored look and nodded. "I trust you'll put the funds to good use. Getting a better wardrobe, perhaps?" She waved her hand. "A craft is waiting outside to take you back to JanIus."

Overwhelmed at the opportunity that sprang into her lap, Mrs. Corral bowed to her again.

"I can't thank you enough, Queen Revari!"

Queen Revari barely noticed her exit. "Send them in," she ordered.

The Overmills cautiously entered the meeting chamber. Mrs. Overmill tried not to panic in the presence of the queen.

"It's my understanding you'd like to keep the triplets permanently. Is that correct?"

"Yes, Your Majesty," said Mrs. Overmill. She cast a furtive glance at her husband. "We understand they have a FatherForm, but they've already endured so much—"

She stopped abruptly when Queen Revari waved her hand in the air. "Pay attention to the TranScreen."

Dutifully, the Overmills looked up at the TranScreen. Mr. Overmill's grip on his wife's hand tightened. A soldier was hogtied and vomiting a foul, reddish substance.

"He helped himself to some of the Callidut we supplied to help Onzi win against planet Baal. Now he's become an addict. I want you to pay close attention to what happens when I'm crossed."

She nodded toward the TranScreen. "Keep watching," she ordered.

Colonel Angela entered the confinement chamber, staring down at the soldier who met her eyes with a blank stare. He didn't have time to utter a sound before she stuck her sword through his chest and cut his heart out.

Mrs. Overmill fought down a wave of nausea. Bile threatened to erupt in her throat as the colonel reached inside his still warm body and removed his heart. She held it high up in the air, toward the nearest surveillance camera. The heart still beat wildly in her small hand.

Queen Revari said, "Due to his treachery, the triplets will be placed under your care permanently. Mrs. Overmill, if I feel my generosity will be repaid with betrayal, I won't hesitate to cut your husband's heart out right in front of you. Have I been heard?"

The Overmills quickly glanced at each other. "Yes, Queen Revari! We won't cause any issues!"

The queen rewarded them with a dazzling half-smile. "ChildForms are a blessing. Have a safe trip back to JanIus."

M rs. Corral could barely contain her excitement as she left Queen Revari's meeting chamber. Imagining all of the things she'd buy with her newly acquired funds made her head swim. Just as she reached the exit of the recreation chamber, her brain was severed from her skull by an Azgoate. She lay motionless on the ground, unaware of a Being turning over her palm and transferring the funds out of her account. She died with a smile frozen on her lips.

After a half-hour had passed, Dr. Azini slammed his fist down on the highly polished table.

"We've been stuck in here for too long! I have things to address back home. How long do they think they can keep us here?"

Dr. Portane looked up at him under bushy eyebrows. "I'm just as ready as you are to go home, but we're not allowed to leave yet. If I were you, I'd be quiet if you don't want to rile Queen Revari."

"Oh no? Why? Are you scared of her, Dr. Portane?" asked Dr. Azini mockingly. He smirked. "Did you see those huge *juggers* sitting up on her chest?"

An older doctor, Dr. Beltzar snickered. "I'd love to push those in my face, eh?"

All the physicians roared with laughter while a horrified Dr. Portane tried desperately to ignore them.

"Yes, that would be nice," said Dr. Azini. "But I prefer WomenForms who don't act like MaleForms. The ones who know their place."

Carving his initials into the table with a scalpel, he said, "The right one hasn't come along to bring Revari down a peg or two.

I hope that day comes. I despise WomenForms like her. If my Fawn thinks she's going to end up like her, I have news for her!"

Colonel Angela entered the chamber. "Dr. Portane, you've been summoned."

Another Revaltian brought in a cart filled with PotterBerry wine and pastries. "Enjoy these refreshments and talk among yourselves until you're called."

With a swift pivot, they exited with Dr. Portane following closely behind them.

Dr. Azini and the other physicians looked around at each other. "Revani has some beautiful WomanForm soldiers," said Dr. Olean.

"Yeah, beautiful and much too full of themselves," muttered Dr. Azini, getting up to pour a glass of wine.

D r. Portane followed Colonel Angela out of the recreation chamber and down the path toward the palace. "Did I do something wrong?" he asked nervously.

"No," she said briskly. "Just keep walking."

D r. Beltzar glared at Dr. Azini. "You gonna hog all that wine, Azini?"

Dr. Azini whirled around and poured another glass. "There's three bottles here, Beltzar. Get off your dusty ass and get it yourself!"

Dr. Beltzar's lip curled in distaste. Before he could stand, a loud explosion roared through the recreation chamber. Flying toward the ceiling with Dr. Azini, he felt his bones breaking. In a fit of desperation, he struggled to breathe through the thick billows of smoke permeating throughout his lungs.

The unrelenting flames ravaged the chamber, leaving him to wonder how he'd been outsmarted by WomenForms.

D r. Portane watched the explosion from Queen Revari's meeting chamber, pulling nervously on his collar.

"By The One! That chamber exploded!"

"It did, didn't it?" asked Queen Revari, never taking her eyes off the carnage.

Shivering, he observed the disaster staff running across the courtyard to extinguish the blaze.

Pivoting swiftly toward him, she said, "That's one way to take out the trash, isn't it?"

Like a cat playing with a mouse, she took a step forward whenever he stepped back. "I think you've been hiding secrets long enough, King Noham. I hear your son is alive and well. You helped him stage his death to avoid getting arrested."

A sharp knee to his crotch sank him to his knees.

"You will tell me where he is, or I'll have you burned alive with your friends."

The savagery in her eyes terrified him. He only hoped his son would stay alive long enough to avenge his death.

Epilogue

He sat staring balefully out of the window, watching the waves crash against the rocks.

A soldier came rushing in and saluted him.

"Your Highness, our surveillance team just located your father! He's on Revani. Queen Revari lured him there under the guise of getting a female physician for the WomenForms. There's been a terrible explosion!"

He frowned at a group of seagulls perched on the cliffs. The soldier took a step back when he turned around to face him. A single blue specked with green eye stared back at the soldier opposite a mass of scars where his other eye used to be.

"Is he dead?"

"I don't know, Your Highness, but—"

"But what?" he snapped. "I'll warn you not to waste my time."

The soldier nodded quickly. "There's more. Queen Revari has a son. He's half-Human, half-MaleForm, and he's on JanIus right now!"

Prince Belial's irritated expression changed to something that chilled the soldier's bones.

"He's on JanIus, not Platirius? Are you certain?"

"Yes, Your Highness!"

"I order you and the surveillance team to find out if my father is still alive. I don't want to hear from you until you know."

The single, sparkling blue eye bore into the soldier. "If you take too long, someone will find you and your mother's bodies in the sea."

The soldier saluted him. "Yes, Your Majesty."

He turned back to the window and touched the grotesque spiderweb of scars covering his left eyelid.

"So you have a son, Queen Revari. You have no idea how many years I've waited to break you. Now, I'll hunt your half-abomination son down and watch you beg me to spare his life. I look forward to taking his eye right in front of you."

His handsome face blazed with rage under the soft rays of the moon.

Justin was cleaning up the last of the supplies he'd used to bandage a wound when he heard the commotion. Since waking up from the coma, he hadn't remembered what had happened before he passed out. After a few weeks had passed, he was finally starting to get back into his old routine.

Dozens of crafts were flying across the sky toward rising smoke. Curiously, he stared out the window, wondering where they were headed. After he washed his hands, the door opened and a young WomanForm entered. He took in her mass of reddish, curly brown hair, light brown eyes, and cinnamon-toned skin.

How did she get past security?

"I'm closed for the night," he told her. "If you come back tomorrow, I'll be able to treat you."

"I'm afraid there's been a misunderstanding, Dr. Ascencio. I'm Dr. Fawn Azini. As of now, I'm taking over my father's practice. You'll be reporting to me."

Justin's eyebrow raised. "Oh? And when did that happen?"

She stared up at him, unfazed by his confusion. "You haven't been listening. Right now. My father perished in the explosion."

"What explosion?"

She raised an eyebrow.

You certainly are clueless for a doctor, aren't you?

"The explosion that just happened on Revani. Everyone is talking about it."

Justin looked out the window again before turning back to look at her.

"Well, that's unfortunate, but King Leighton appointed me. He's still the authority on JanIus."

"He may be the king, but this was my father's practice. Now it's mine. If you have reservations about taking orders from a WomanForm, you're welcome to move on."

Justin smirked. "I have no issues with WomenForms, but I do have a problem with arrogance."

159

He cocked his head. "That's something you and your father seem to have in common."

Her steely glare didn't intimidate him. After witnessing how brutal Queen Revari could be, the ire of all other females paled in comparison.

She shrugged. "I don't care what you think of me, but I expect you to stay out of my way. Good night, Dr. Ascencio."

Justin unfolded his arms and caught her arm.

She looked down at his hand, then up at his face. "Get your hand off me."

"Only after you answer a question, if you don't mind?"

She snatched her arm away from him. "I don't like being touched, nor do I answer to you."

He stepped around her, blocking the entrance. "That's fine, but I'm sure you'll have a good answer for what I'm about to ask."

She blew out an exasperated sigh and folded her arms.

"One question. Then you'll move or I'll move you. Is that clear?"

Justin smiled down at her.

I'd love to see you try, Dr. Azini.

"My apologies. Actually, I have two questions. Why did you come to Earth to save me, and why did you make sure I followed you to JanIus?"

Author Bio

D.L. Hannah was born in Youngstown, Ohio. She is a writer, entrepreneur, and host of the Amerisogyny podcast. She is a Psi Chi and Alpha Kappa Delta member and earned a Bachelor of Arts degree in Clinical-Community Psychology from Walsh University. For over twenty years, she has been a strong advocate for children diagnosed with Autism. She now lives in North Carolina with her family.

Join my VIP list

Join my VIP list @ www.dlhannah.com

Also by D.L. Hannah

Platirius: Infiltration Book I
Platirius: The Rise of Reve Book II
Platirius: Kikhani vs Platirius Book III
Coldarius: The Origin of Gallium Book I
Coldarius: The Betrayal Book II
JanIus: Pawns Book I
JanIus: Enter the King Book II
JanIus: Platirius vs JanIus Book III
Maieman: Paradox Book I
Maieman: Revelations Book II

References

The New York Times (1971, July 25). Rome Woman Miscarries With Total of 15 Fetuses
https://www.nytimes.com/1971/07/25/archives/rome-woman
-miscarries-with-total-of-15-fetuses.html

National Post Staff (2022, Jun 25, Updated 2022 Jun 27).
Woman with rare medical condition gives birth to 44 kids by age 40
https://nationalpost.com/news/world/woman-with-rare-medi
cal-condition-gives-birth-to-44-kids-by-age-40

Elder, A. G., Sosa Gama, A. M., De Gasperi, R. (2010 Jan-Feb;77(1): 69–81). Transgenic Mouse Models of Alzheimer's Disease
National Library of Medicine: National Center for Biotechnology Information
https://pmc.ncbi.nlm.nih.gov/articles/PMC2925685/